KISSES FROM HELL

ADDITIONAL HELL COLLECTIONS:

Prom Nights from Hell

Love Is Hell

Vacations from Hell

Kisses from Hell

KRISTIN CAST

ALYSON NOËL

KELLEY ARMSTRONG

RICHELLE MEAD

FRANCESCA LIA BLOCK

HARPER TEEN

An Imprint of HarperCollins*Publishers*

HarperTeen is an imprint of HarperCollins Publishers.

Library of Congress Cataloging-in-Publication Data

Kisses from hell / Kristin Cast ... [et al.]. — 1st ed.

v. cm.

Summary: Five stories of teen vampire romance.

Contents: Sunshine / Richelle Mead — Bring me to life / Alyson Noel — Alone / Kristin Cast — Hunting Kat / Kelley Armstrong — Lilith / Francesca Lia Block.

ISBN 978-0-06-195697-3 (trade bdg.) — ISBN 978-0-06-195696-6 (pbk. bdg.)

1. Vampires—Juvenile fiction. 2. Love stories, American. 3. Love stories, Canadian. 4. Short stories, American. 5. Short stories, Canadian. [1. Vampires—Fiction. 2. Love—Fiction. 3. Short stories.] I. Cast, Kristin.

PZ5.K59535 2010   2010009734

[Fic]—dc22   CIP

                                                                              AC

Typography by Amy Ryan

10   11   12   13   14   CG/RRDB   10   9   8   7   6   5   4   3   2

❖

First Edition

COLLEGESUMMIT.
LET TALENT SHINE

A portion of the proceeds from the sale of this collection will be donated to College Summit, a national nonprofit organization that partners with school districts to increase the college enrollment rate of all students, particularly those from low-income backgrounds.

ABOUT COLLEGE ACCESS IN AMERICA

- Every year, 200,000 students who have the ability to go to college do not enroll.
- Low-income students who get As on standardized tests go to college at the same rate as the top-income students who get Ds.

WHAT COLLEGE SUMMIT IS DOING TO HELP SEND MORE STUDENTS TO COLLEGE

College Summit believes that sending one young person to college improves his or her life; sending a group of young people to college can improve a community; but making the college-going process work for all young people can transform our nation.

Since 1993, College Summit has reached more than 35,000 students and trained more than 700 high school teachers in college application management. Additionally, 79% of high school juniors who attend a College Summit workshop enroll in college, nearly double the national average of 46% for low-income high school graduates—an achievement that helps these students break the cycle of poverty in their families forever.

To learn more about College Summit, and for tips on what you can do to prepare yourself for college or encourage others, visit www.collegesummit.org.

Sunshine

RICHELLE MEAD

One

*E*mma wasn't Eric Dragomir's first girlfriend. Nor was she likely to be his last.

Of course, the latter statement was assuming Eric's father didn't interfere. As far as old Frederick Dragomir was concerned, Eric and Emma should have already been married. It was a wonder, Eric thought bitterly, that his father hadn't simply planned on having the wedding the same day they graduated high school.

"What's the problem? How many more girls are you going to go through?" Frederick had demanded the last time father and son had visited. "She's from a good family. Pretty. Smart. Nice enough. What more do you want? I know you think you're too young, but time's running out! There's hardly any of us left."

Standing now on a Chilean beach that felt light-years

away from Montana, watching the stars flicker against a deep purple sky, Eric wondered if that was what had driven his parents to get married. Fear that their kind was dwindling away. He'd never thought much about their relationship while he was growing up. They were just his parents. They existed. They would always be together. They would always be around. He'd taken that for granted, never pondering the more intimate feelings within their marriage. He realized, now that his mother was gone, that he hadn't even really taken the time to get to know them as people. It was too late for her, and lately, with all the marriage pressure, Eric really wasn't all that excited to learn much more about his father.

Emma appeared suddenly, like an apparition, linking her arm with his. "Aren't you glad the sun went down? That light was literally killing me."

Eric didn't bother to correct her misuse of "literally"— or to tell her that he didn't mind the sun, even though too much exposure irritated their kind. In fact, he always kind of regretted that they—as living vampires— couldn't handle much of the light. He sometimes entertained fantasies of lying by a pool, wrapped in the sun's golden embrace.

Instead he smiled down at Emma, taking in her long-lashed deep blue eyes and elaborately braided dark brown hair. The eyes and hair contrasted sharply with that pale, porcelain skin all Moroi had. Combined with her heart-shaped face and high cheekbones, Emma Drozdov made lots of guys stop and stare—Eric included.

You were wrong again, Dad, Eric thought. *She isn't pretty. She's stunning.*

Maybe settling down with Emma wouldn't be such a bad thing. They always had a good time together, and his father had been right about her being nice and smart. She'd also demonstrated—on more than one occasion—her willingness and creativity when it came to certain physical acts. Life with her would never be boring, and Eric suspected she was as eager as his father for an engagement ring.

"Hey," she said with a nudge. "What's up? Why are you all serious?"

He groped for an answer that wouldn't betray how moody he was—or how he kept going back and forth on their relationship. What else had his father said last time? *You can't wait forever. What if something happens to you? What'll become of us then?*

"Just pissed off at how long the boat's taking," Eric said at last, silencing his father's nagging voice. "We were supposed to get out of here before sunset."

"I know," she said, her gaze scanning the area. Around them stood the other members of their graduating class—well, the *elite* members of their class. They were milling and chatting, waiting eagerly to board the yacht that would ferry them to what was supposedly the party of the year. "And now they're taking forever."

"The crew has to load supplies," Eric pointed out. The boat had been tied up against a dock for a while as food and luggage were loaded. Weary-looking feeders—humans who willingly gave blood to Moroi vampires—were now being marched up the dock and onto the boat. Really, simply using the yacht for transport seemed like a waste. It was newly built and, according to rumor, filled with all sorts of luxury accommodations. Even in the fading light, the boat gleamed a brilliant white. Some might consider it small for a yacht, but it could have easily housed his class for a weeklong party.

"Still, we should have left an hour ago." Emma's eyes fell on Jared Zeklos—a royal whose father was behind the weekend-long celebration. She smirked, fangs just barely showing against her glossy red lips. "Jared acted so full of himself when this party was announced. Now people are going to turn on him."

It was true. That was the nature of the circle they existed in. Eric almost felt sorry for the guy, who was clearly uncomfortable as the annoyed gazes of his class-mates ran over him. "Well, I'm sure it's not his—"

A scream cut the hum of chatter and laughter. Eric jerked toward the sound, instinctively pulling Emma against him. The beach and dock were in a fairly deserted area—as so many Moroi territories were—accessible only by a narrow dirt road cutting through a jungle that had hardly been touched by human or vampire hands.

And there, just near the tree line, Eric saw a face straight from his nightmares. A person—no, creature—was lunging toward a red-haired girl. The creature's face was pale, but not in the manner of the Moroi. It had a sickly, chalky pallor. Eric could scarcely believe it, but he knew: It was one of the Strigoi, undead vampires who killed those they took blood from. They didn't live and breed the way Moroi did. They were unnatural creatures who transformed from the living into a twisted, undead state. Sometimes, a Moroi could do this by choice if they drank all the blood of a victim. Other times, Strigoi were made forcefully when a Strigoi bit a victim and then fed Strigoi blood back. Really, the means of creation didn't matter. Strigoi were lethal, with no sense of their previous lives. The paleness of the Strigoi's face was that of death and decay, and Eric knew that up close, the Strigoi's pupils would be ringed in red.

Snarling, the Strigoi aimed its fangs at the girl's neck, and he was moving with a speed that didn't seem physically possible. Eric had been taught about Strigoi his entire life, but nothing could have prepared him for the real thing. Emma apparently wasn't prepared either, judging from the way she was clinging to him and digging her fingers into his arms. More screaming filled the air, and Eric caught sight of yet another Strigoi leaping out of the shadows and moving to the new Moroi graduates. Panic surged through the group, followed by the inevitable chaos that came whenever people were trapped and terrified. Trampling seemed inevitable.

Then, almost as quickly as the Strigoi had burst out, new figures suddenly emerged from the crowd. Their clothing was similar to that of Eric's classmates, but there was no confusing them with the Moroi. They were dhampirs—guardians, to be specific—the half-human, half-vampire warriors who guarded Moroi. Shorter and more muscular than the living vampires they protected, the guardians had trained and honed their reflexes to as close to the Strigoi's as possible. There were almost a dozen guardians on the beach and just two Strigoi. The guardians wasted no time in taking advantage of their numbers.

The scene lasted only a few moments, and yet Eric felt like he was watching it in slow motion. The guardians—who had been dispersed among the waiting group—split their forces and went after each Strigoi. The one attacking the red-haired girl was ripped away from her and staked before he could do any damage. The other Strigoi never even got a chance to go for a victim before he was taken down.

It took a few minutes for the crowd to settle down and see that the danger was gone. A great cheer went up when they realized what had happened, and suddenly it was as though the whole thing had been a nonevent. A few of the guardians dragged away the bodies of the staked Strigoi to be burned while the rest began shouting that the Moroi needed to be loaded onto the boat *now*. Herded along, Eric walked in a daze toward the dock, still trying to process what had happened.

Despite the cheers, a number of his classmates wore expressions mirroring how he felt. These were Moroi who had either run into Strigoi before or at least respected the risks. The rest of the group, having spent a good of part of their lives in the safety of their well-guarded school, had never seen a Strigoi. Sure, they'd been raised with all the stories, but the quick dispatch of these Strigoi had unfortunately diminished some people's fears. It was a naive and dangerous mistake.

"Did you see that?" exclaimed Emma. Despite her initial terror, she, too, seemed to be joining those letting down their guard. "Those Strigoi were there, and then *bam*! The guardians just took them out! What were they thinking? The Strigoi, I mean. They were totally outnumbered."

Eric didn't point out the obvious to her. Strigoi didn't care about those kinds of odds—mostly because half the time, the odds didn't matter. It had taken only two Strigoi to slaughter his mother and the group she'd been with, which had included six guardians. In a lot of situations, six would have been more than enough guardians. For her, it hadn't been, and Eric was a bit surprised that Emma was so caught up in the sensational nature of the moment that she'd forgotten about his family history.

Since his mother's death, he had seen the Strigoi all the time in his nightmares, nightmares that no one ever seemed to want to hear about. That the creatures in his nightmares had not matched his recent reality didn't seem to make a difference. For a moment, he could hardly walk, so consumed was he by the memory of that horrible, snarling face. Was that what it had been like for his mother? Had she been attacked as suddenly and brutally? No warning . . . just fangs ripping out her neck. . . . His classmate had been pulled away just before those lethal teeth could make contact. His mother hadn't been so lucky.

"Everyone's talking to Ashley," grumbled Emma, nodding toward where several people were gathered around the almost-victim as they boarded the boat. "I want to know what it was like."

Awful, thought Eric. *Terrifying.* Yet Ashley seemed to be thriving on the attention. And the rest of their classmates were wound up and excited—as though the Strigoi attack had been staged as pre-entertainment for their party. He stared around dumbfounded. How could none of them take this seriously? The Strigoi had been picking off Moroi for centuries. How could no one remember his mother's death—which had only been six months ago? How could *Emma* not remember that? She wasn't a cruel person, but he was a bit appalled at how oblivious she was to his feelings after the "excitement."

Maybe he shouldn't have been surprised. His own father didn't appear to remember the past half the time. Everyone seemed to think Eric should be done mourning and ready to move on. That was certainly what his father thought. Eric sometimes wondered if his father's fixation with Eric getting married young had taken the place of true mourning. Frederick Dragomir was obsessed with saving his royal bloodline, which was now down to only two people, father and son.

Emma grinned up at Eric, the half-moon's light making her eyes shine. They suddenly seemed a little less beautiful to him than they had before. "Wasn't that crazy?" she asked. "I can't wait to see what happens next!"

Two

*R*hea Daniels didn't like boats. She'd always wondered if it had something to do with being a fire wielder. All Moroi used magic tied to one of the four elements—earth, air, water, or fire. Those who used water always seemed to love swimming and being in boats. Not Rhea. The rocking back and forth—even on a large boat like this—made her nauseous, and she had a recurrent fear of falling over the side and sinking into a cold, dark grave.

That didn't stop her from standing near the edge tonight, far from the laughter of the others who were still going on about the attack on the beach. She didn't mind the isolation; she didn't know most of them any-way. Besides, the yacht's outer sides received the most wind, and that cooling air made her feel a little less sick. Nonetheless, she still gripped the railing with a tightness that made her fingers cramp. Grimacing, she glanced ahead at their destination. Like all vampires, she had excellent night vision and could discern the island's dark shape against the star-clustered sky. They weren't moving nearly fast enough toward it, as far as she was concerned.

"Don't your hands hurt?"

The voice startled her. Moroi had good hearing, too, but the newcomer had caught her off guard. Glancing over, she saw a guy watching her curiously as he shoved his hands into khaki pants. The wind was making a mess of his pale blond hair, but he didn't seem to notice. That hair color was fascinating. Her own was a light shade of gold, but his was a platinum that would probably look white in the right lighting. There was also a regal air to him, like someone who'd been born and bred to power and prestige, but that description applied to most everyone on this trip.

"No," she lied. Silence fell. Rhea hated silence. She always felt the need to make conversation and struggled now to think of what to say next. "Why are you over here?" The words came out harsh, and she winced.

He gave her a small smile. He had nice lips, she decided. "Do you want me to leave? Is this your private part of the ship?"

"No, no, of course not." She hoped he couldn't see

her blush in the dark. "I just thought . . . I mean, I'm just surprised you aren't with everyone else."

She thought he might make some teasing remark, but then, to her surprise, the smile vanished. He averted his eyes and stared out to sea. She studied his clothes as he did. He wasn't in a tux or anything, but the slacks and sweater screamed wealth and status. She felt self-conscious in her jeans. His next words brought her back from her fashion analysis.

"I guess I'm just tired of hearing the Strigoi stories," he said at last, voice stiff. "Like how it was some kind of awesome sideshow."

"Ah." She glanced back to where that girl—Ashley?—was recounting her tale for the hundredth time. Rhea kept hearing snatches of it, and the story seemed to grow more elaborate with each telling. In this version, the Strigoi had actually thrown her to the ground, and all the guardians had been needed to rescue her. Rhea returned her attention to her odd companion. "Yeah . . . I don't really find that interesting—at least not the way they do."

"You don't?" He turned back to her, eyes widening as though it was the strangest thing in the world that someone wouldn't think a Strigoi attack was cool. She saw then that his eyes were jade-colored, as fascinating to her as his hair. That shade of green was beautiful and rare, only showing up in a few of the royal families. The

Dashkovs were one, but she couldn't recall the others.

"Of course not," she scoffed, hoping her scrutiny of him hadn't been too obvious. "They wouldn't be so excited if someone had actually been hurt. I mean, God, don't they remember that attack earlier this year in San Jose? When all those people died?"

The guy's posture went rigid, his eyes still wide, and she suddenly regretted her words. Had he known one of the victims? She felt stupid and awkward, silently berating herself for not thinking before she spoke.

"I'm sorry—I shouldn't have—"

"You remember that?" he asked, his voice as puzzled as before.

"Yes . . . how couldn't I? I mean . . . well, I didn't know anyone personally, but all those people . . . most were Lazars, but there was that Szelsky lord . . . and Prince Dragomir's wife. What was her name?"

"Alma," he said softly, still regarding her wonderingly.

Rhea hesitated, not sure how much she should say about it. She was certain now that he'd known someone. "Well, it was horrible. Beyond horrible. I can't even imagine how their families must feel. . . ."

"It was six months ago," he said abruptly.

Rhea frowned, trying to figure out the meaning in that statement. He wasn't brushing it off or implying that six months was a long time—which, in her opinion, it wasn't. He spoke as though he was testing her, which didn't make much sense.

"I don't think six months is a long enough time to get over losing someone you love," she said at last. "I know I couldn't. Did—did you know anyone there?"

He opened his mouth to say something, but a sudden wave jolted the boat. It lurched slightly, causing a few eager squeals from the crowd beyond them. Rhea gasped and squeezed the rail harder—which she honestly hadn't thought was even possible—and lost her footing a little. Her companion caught hold of her, helping her stay steady as the boat righted itself and regained its smooth sailing.

Deep breaths, deep breaths, she told herself. Wasn't that what people did to calm themselves? Heavy breathing didn't seem to be a problem for her. She was on the verge of hyperventilating, and her heart felt like it was going to pound right out of her chest.

"Easy," he said, voice low and soothing. "You're okay. It was just a bad wave."

Rhea couldn't answer. Her body remained taut and locked, unable to move or react in her terror.

"Hey," he tried again. "Everything's fine. Look—we're almost there, see?"

With much effort, Rhea turned to where he nodded. Sure enough, the island was much closer. A cluster of lights marked the dock, and figures along the shore seemed ready to guide them in.

Exhaling, she relaxed her grip—a tiny bit—and shifted her body. He still held on to her, apparently unsure if she really was okay.

"Thank you," she managed at last. "I'm . . . I'm fine now."

He waited a few more moments and then finally released her. As he lifted his hand from where it had been pressed against one of hers, he seemed surprised to notice the ring she wore. Its large marquise-cut diamond glittered like a star on her finger. He stared at it in shock as though she was wearing a cobra wrapped around her hand.

"Are you . . . are you engaged?"

"To Stephen Badica."

"Seriously?"

The tone of his voice—his complete sense of disbelief—suddenly triggered a fierce spark of anger in her. Of course he was surprised. Why wouldn't he be? Everyone else was. They all wondered how it was possible that Rhea Daniels—who was only *half*-royal— could have caught the interest of someone who came from such a prestigious branch of his line. Her parents' marriage had been a big enough scandal. Everyone had thought her mother married beneath her, and Rhea knew the sting of that was what had caused her mother to encourage this engagement to Stephen.

Still, Rhea hated the insinuations. She'd heard the whispers; she knew people who wondered if maybe her parents had cut some kind of deal with Stephen's parents, some bribe. Others said that Stephen was interested because she was easy—and that the engagement wouldn't last once he tired of her. She knew they seemed like a weird match. Rhea was quiet—more of an observer of the world. Stephen was outgoing and boisterous, always at the center of the world—so much so that he was off now with the others, reliving the earlier excitement.

Rhea stepped back from the blond guy. "Yes," she said crisply. "Seriously. He's great. He invited me along." She was one of the few people here who hadn't attended St. Vladimir's Academy.

"Yeah . . ." This guy didn't sound entirely sure. Mostly, he still seemed baffled. "I just . . . I just can't see you guys together."

Of course not. He was obviously someone very elite. Even among royalty, there were those who were better than others. It was honestly a wonder he was even talking to her.

"Don't you worry . . . don't you worry you're too young?" Again, he carried that wondering tone, further incensing her.

"When you've found someone good, you don't need to jump from person to person."

He flinched and seemed to fumble for a response, making her wonder if she'd hit a sensitive area. He was saved when a pretty brown-haired girl called to him to come join them. She addressed him as Eric.

"You'd better go," said Rhea. "It was nice talking to you."

He started to turn and then hesitated once more. "What's your name?"

"Rhea Daniels."

"Rhea . . ." He said the name as though he was ana-lyzing each syllable. "I'm Eric."

"Yeah, I heard." She stared back over the boat's edge, signaling that she was done talking to him. She had the impression he might say something more, but after sev-eral heavy seconds, she could just make out the sound of him walking away as the waves crashed alongside the boat.

Three

Everyone was ready to party as soon as they stepped off the dock. Despite the black sky, it was midday for the Moroi—a bit early for revelry, but no one seemed to care. And after everyone caught their first glimpse of the Zeklos beach house, it was easy to forgive Jared for the late start. Even Eric was in awe, and he'd been surrounded by luxury his entire life. The giant estate sprawled on a small bluff, the entire building covered in windows that promised a spectacular view from almost anywhere inside. Exotic trees partially covered the property, making it difficult for passing boats to discern many details. Moroi interacted with humans all the time but still sought out privacy when possible. Far beyond the house, on the other side of the island, were some rocky cliffs.

The guardians made everyone stay on the yacht while a safety sweep of the island was performed. Most of Eric's classmates grumbled about this, Emma included. No one seemed to think Strigoi could have infiltrated the island, but Eric knew it was just as easy for Strigoi to get in a boat as anyone else. Jared's father had his own guardians on the grounds, but that didn't mean Strigoi couldn't have slipped in on a previous night.

Eric was still a little disgusted at everyone's flippant attitude about the Strigoi, but other thoughts pushed the disapproval to the back of his mind. Like Rhea Daniels.

Why had she gotten so mad at him? He'd replayed their conversation over and over, trying to figure out what he might have said. The only thing he could guess was that she'd taken some offense over his surprise about her being with Stephen. Maybe she'd thought Eric was insulting Stephen. That hadn't been Eric's intent— though he still believed the two were an unlikely couple. Stephen was always loud, always drawing attention to himself and making people laugh. Maybe opposites really did attract, but Eric thought it was telling that he'd never heard of Stephen having a fiancée until now. Of course, since they'd all just graduated, the engagement could have been a recent event.

In fact, thinking back to their wait on the beach, Eric recalled seeing Stephen telling jokes and entertaining the others. Rhea hadn't been nearby. Or had she been?

Maybe Eric had just overlooked her—not that that seemed possible. How could anyone overlook her? Even now, faced with the tantalizing prospect of parties to come, Eric found his mind consumed with his memories of her. The soft, golden blond hair that seemed so much more alive than his own, almost like the forbidden sunshine he so longed for. The faint scattering of freckles across her pale skin—a rarity among the Moroi. And the eyes . . . her eyes were a rich hazel, flecked with green and gold. There had been something infinitely wise and kind in those eyes, particularly when she'd spoken about the massacre. She hadn't known anyone in it, but it had still pained her.

"Finally," said Emma. The guardians were ushering the Moroi onto the dock and up into the island. "I can't *wait* to see what kind of rooms we have. Miranda was here once and said they're huge."

They were indeed, but Eric didn't spend much time in his. Moroi servants—nonroyals, of course—carried in the guests' baggage and made sure everyone knew where their room assignments were. Enormous it might be, but the house couldn't provide thirty bedrooms, so some people had to share. Eric was one of the lucky ones who had his own, which didn't surprise him. With his father's status and power, most royals wanted to get in good with him. Jared's family would be no exception.

After that brief stop, everyone spilled out toward the

back of the house, where the Zeklos servants had been hard at work. In a secluded, tiled area bordered by sheltering trees, tall torches were staked into the ground, lighting up the darkness with eerie, flickering light. The scents of roasting meat and other delicacies filled the air, and in the center of it all was a man-made lagoon, its water a deep, crystalline blue that was lit from within by cleverly embedded lights. The entire pool glowed like something otherworldly.

Jared's father, a thin man with slanting black eyebrows and a waxed mustache, gave a brief speech congratulating them on their graduation from high school and wishing them luck on whatever roads they chose to follow. When he finished, the festivities kicked in immediately. Music blared from unseen speakers, and all thoughts of future responsibility and important plans were quickly forgotten.

Eric threw himself into the drinking and dancing, suddenly wanting nothing more than to forget everything for a while. He didn't want to think about his mother or that awful, nightmarish face down on the beach. He didn't want to think about the legacy left to him, of being the heir to a dying royal line. He didn't want to think about his father's plans for him. And above all, Eric most certainly didn't want to think about the solemn girl he'd met on the boat. Sometimes he found parties like this trite, but other times . . . well, in the hardest moments of his life, crazy revelry was a welcome escape.

"This is the most fun you've been in a while," exclaimed Emma, shouting to be heard over the music.

Eric grinned and pulled her close to him with one arm as they danced. His other hand was precariously holding a drink—and not doing a very good job of it. Considering it was his third, it probably didn't matter if he lost some.

"You don't think I'm usually fun?" he teased.

Emma shook her head. "No . . . you've just been so serious lately. Like you're nervous about . . . I don't know. Nervous about the future." She knocked back some of her own drink and frowned prettily. "Are you?"

It was a surprisingly pensive moment for her, and Eric wasn't sure how to respond. Emma was usually all about living in the now, about seeking as much fun and excitement as she could—without thinking of the consequences. It was one of the things he liked best about her when his own worries plagued him.

"I don't know," he admitted, deciding he needed to finish his own drink if this conversation was going to continue. Both the music and topic made it difficult to continue. "There's just so much pressure . . . so many decisions that could affect the rest of my life."

Emma stood up on her tiptoes and gave him a quick

kiss. "Just because you have to make a decision doesn't mean it's going to have bad consequences. And some of us don't mind standing with you through it all."

Through his haze of vodka martinis, he heard a subtle hint about their engagement in her statement. Eric decided then that he wished they hadn't strayed onto this topic. He was going to suggest another drink, but a distraction of a different kind popped up.

"And now," a voice declared, managing to carry over the heavy bass of the music, "I will attempt a feat never, ever before attempted by anyone in history. Not *ever*."

Eric and Emma turned, finding Stephen Badica standing on a chair by the edge of the pool. Everyone in his vicinity stopped what they were doing to watch. Even without his theatrics, Stephen often drew eyes. He had a build that was a bit brawnier than the typically slim Moroi figure, giving him a look he joked was "rugged and manly." He didn't have pretty-boy features, but the strong lines of his chiseled face met with the approval of most girls—especially since he always seemed to be smiling.

Stephen held up a shot glass. "I'm going to jump into the pool and finish this shot before I hit the water."

This was met with cheers and whistles, as well as the cries of a few naysayers protesting that he'd be spilling whiskey in the water. Stephen held up his free hand as though calling for silence—impossible in this situation—and then leaped off the chair. It all happened fast, but Eric was pretty sure he saw Stephen actually down the shot before hitting the water—in his clothes—cannonball-style. Water exploded everywhere, and there were a few squeals of surprise as several people got soaked. Emma was among them, her slinky red dress catching a particularly large wave.

More cheers erupted from the spectators, and Stephen emerged from the pool holding up his hands in victory. After a few whoops of joy, he then challenged others to do it. Naturally, there were several volunteers.

Watching Stephen, Eric realized he wasn't going to be able to push aside all his cares tonight. There was a part of him that kept secretly hoping he'd see sunny blond hair in the crowd. Turning to Emma, who was futilely trying to wring water out of her skirt, he asked, "Hey, do you know anything about Stephen being engaged?"

"Huh?" Emma's eyes were still on her skirt. "Oh, yeah. To some girl from . . . I don't remember. Some other school. She's here somewhere—she's got blond hair. Kind of quiet. Why?"

Eric shrugged. "I just heard about it earlier and was surprised that Stephen was engaged. I never thought he was the settling down type."

Emma gave up on her dress and looked back up.

"More like he doesn't seem the type to settle down with *her*."

"What? Why? What's wrong with her?"

"She's only half-royal." Emma couldn't keep the scorn out of her voice. "Her mom's an Ozera, I think, but her dad's a nobody."

"That's kind of harsh."

"Hey, I've got nothing against her. And she's done pretty good to snag Stephen. Nice work there. That's definitely going to bring her up in the world." Emma tugged at Eric's shirt, Stephen and Rhea already forgotten. "Come on. My dress is ruined."

"Huh? What are you—"

Maybe it was the abrupt change in topic—or just too much to drink—but Eric wasn't able to stop Emma when she jerked him toward the pool. They landed ungracefully, sending more water up over the edge and onto the patterned tile. Other people had already followed Stephen's example, and Eric thought it a miracle he hadn't landed on anyone already in the pool.

"Ugh," he said, looking down at his waterlogged clothes. Emma laughed in triumph and threw her arms around him.

"Gotcha," she said.

He started to complain but soon discovered it was hard to with Emma pressed up against him. Uncaring of the others around, she kissed him, and Eric found the feel of her body, with its tightly clinging dress, was better than alcohol for forgetting his worries. He jerked her closer, running his hand over her hip.

"You want to call it an early night?" she asked huskily, breaking the kiss at last.

Eric hesitated, thinking that might be a very good idea. Then, out of the corner of his eye, he caught the longed-for glimpse of shining gold hair. Rhea Daniels was here after all. She slipped inside the house's elaborate glass doors, but not before her eyes flicked over to him. On her face, he saw . . . what? Disapproval? Scorn? He wasn't sure, but suddenly, inexplicably, he knew he had to talk to her.

Reluctantly pulling away from Emma, he got his first good look at just how much her wet dress revealed. "I want to stay," he said, forcing what he hoped was a reckless smile. "But not in these clothes."

She tried to draw him back. "Want me to help take them off?"

"Later," he said, kissing her forehead. He began climbing out of the pool. "I'm going to change. Be right back."

Emma pouted, but as he'd suspected, she felt no need to put on dry clothes, despite the chill in the air. She didn't mind showing off her body to others and would no doubt tolerate the cold in exchange for attention. "Fine, but don't take long." He helped her out. "I'm getting another drink."

Once she was on her way to the bar, Eric hurried inside the house, hoping he could find Rhea in its labyrinthine setup. Others wandered through, either chatting or seeking privacy, but there was no sign of Rhea. He passed the kitchen, filled with bustling staff who were still working hard to keep up with the demand for appetizers and liquor. Frustrated, he pulled someone aside and asked if she'd seen anyone matching Rhea's description.

"Sure," said the serving girl. "She went toward the feeders."

Eric offered his thanks and ran toward the wing of the house she directed him to. Visiting feeders at a party like this was strange. Sometimes feeders were actually kept in the middle of a party, but with the estate's setup, getting blood meant leaving the festivities. Most people—including Eric—had fed beforehand.

Moving quickly, he reached the entrance to the feeders' room just as Rhea was about to go inside. Hearing his footfall, she paused in the doorway. Those golden-green eyes widened in surprise. She'd changed out of her earlier jeans into a clingy green cashmere dress that seemed both demure and sexy to him. Seeing her in full light now, he was astonished at just how beautiful she was. And that hair, oh that hair.

He came to a halt, suddenly realizing he had no clue what it was he wanted to say.

Four

"Whtat are you doing here?" he asked after an uneasy silence.

Rhea stared. That Eric guy was the last person she'd expected to see down in the feeders' area, especially considering he'd just been making out with the brunette in the pool minutes before. It was only the totally stupid nature of his question that allowed her to quickly gather herself. Rhea put one hand on her hip.

"What do you think?" she responded.

"Er, yeah . . . I mean, I know why you're here, but . . ." He was clearly struggling to save himself here, and she wondered how much he'd had to drink. "But I mean, it just seems kind of weird at a party."

"I can't have blood before I get on a boat. Otherwise I get sick." She reconsidered. "Sicker."

"Oh. Yeah. That makes sense."

Another awkward pause hung between them. Finally Rhea turned toward the room. "Now that the interrogation's over, can I go eat?"

"Sure . . . sure. Do you mind if I . . . if I hang out with you?"

Rhea couldn't keep the surprise off her face as she tried to figure out why he would want to stay with her. Earlier on the boat, he'd obviously looked down on her the same way everyone else did for her flawed pedigree. Why show interest now? Not wanting to seem like she cared too much one way or another, she simply entered the room and called back, "Sure."

There was a Moroi attendant on duty who seemed as surprised as Eric that she was there. The guy marked her off on the list that tracked how often Moroi fed and looked astonished when she asked how he was doing tonight. Rhea had a feeling that most of the royals around here tended to treat the servants like furniture.

"Can I have Dennis?" she asked. "Is he awake?"

The attendant was much more cheerful, now that she'd behaved civilly. "Yup. He's the last one on the right."

Rhea smiled and thanked him before walking down the rows of cubicles that sequestered the feeders. At a busier feeding time, all the spaces would have been full, but with the party going on, only a few of the cubicles

were occupied. Some of the humans read while waiting for Moroi to come by; others simply stared off into
space, blissfully gone on the high of a vampire bite. It
was the rush all these humans lived for. They'd been
taken from the fringes of human society, outcasts and
homeless who were more than happy to give their blood
in exchange for the ecstasy it brought. The Moroi also
took care of them, giving the humans plenty of food and
comfortable accommodations.

"Who's Dennis?" asked Eric, walking beside Rhea.
He smelled like chlorine and was dripping puddles with
each step. Nonetheless, she still found him oddly attrac-
tive, which frustrated her.

"He's a feeder who came from my school," she
explained. She couldn't help a small smile when she
thought of Dennis. "He's sweet. He always asks for me
to come back to him."

The look Eric gave her told her that he thought it
was all ridiculous. Her smile vanished, and she quickened her pace to Dennis's cubicle. Dennis was one of the
humans simply content to stare off and do nothing until
his next fix. But as soon as he saw her, he straightened to
attention, nearly leaping out of his chair.

"Rhea!" he exclaimed. "I thought you'd forgotten
me. It's been so long."

Rhea sat down in the chair beside him. She felt the
smile creeping back to her lips. He was only a little older

than her, but there was something cute and childlike about him. She always wanted to pat his messy brown hair back into place.

"It hasn't been that long," she said. "It's only been a day."

Dennis frowned, apparently trying to decide if that was true or not. It was easy for feeders to lose track of time. His eyes lifted to where Eric leaned against the cubicle's entrance. Dennis's enraptured look changed to a frown.

"Who's that?" Dennis asked suspiciously.

"That's Eric," she said soothingly. "He's . . . my friend." Was he? She wasn't sure, but it was best not to agitate Dennis.

"I don't like him," Dennis declared. "He has weird eyes."

"I like his eyes," Rhea said, still trying to be gentle. "They're neat."

Dennis turned back to her, and seeing her face, his expression softened. He sighed happily. "I like *your* eyes. They're beautiful. Like you."

She shook her head ruefully. She was used to his dreamy behavior, but Eric seemed offended by it. Like so many, he regarded feeders as objects. "Come on," she said. "Let's do this."

Dennis eagerly tilted his neck, giving her full access. The skin there might have been smooth once, but now it was covered with the faint bruises of constant biting. Still, Rhea had no trouble sinking her fangs into his flesh and drinking the warm, sweet blood that was as essential to her survival as the solid food she ate. Dennis managed a small, happy sigh, and both of them shared a minute or so of total joy.

When she finished and pulled away, Dennis turned to her with bright, ecstatic eyes. "You don't have to stop," he said. "You can take more."

He always made that offer, but Moroi were trained from an early age about the strict limits to how much they could take. It was what allowed these humans to survive the constant feedings. Plus, limitations steered Moroi away from that ultimate sin: Becoming a Strigoi by drinking all of a person's blood.

Rhea wiped her mouth and rose. Dennis started to stand as well and then sank back down, addled by the dizziness that usually followed a feeding. "Will you come back?" he pleaded. "Soon?"

"I'll be back as soon as I always am," she said. "Tomorrow."

Dennis looked unhappy about this, like usual, but reluctantly nodded in acceptance as she left. Eric followed in her wake, thoughtful and quiet, but suddenly burst out at her the second they stepped back into the hall.

"Are you crazy?" he asked.

Startled, she stopped so quickly that he bumped into her. They both froze at that contact, and then he hastily stepped back.

"What are you talking about?" she asked.

Eric pointed at the door. "That. That guy's out of his mind."

"He's a feeder," she replied. "They're all kind of that way."

"No. He's different. He's obsessed with you."

"He just knows me, that's all. I told you—he's from my school. I've been talking to him and feeding from him for the last couple of years."

"*That's* the problem."

"What, feeding?"

Eric shook his head. "No. Talking to him. You should just get your blood and go."

Rhea couldn't believe she'd almost been reconsidering her first impression of Eric. "Oh, of course. Feeders aren't people to you, right? Not worthy of your notice unless they're part of your royal world?"

"No! I just think you're encouraging him to . . . I don't know. The way he looked at you. He doesn't seem . . . safe."

"He's fine," she argued. "He's a feeder. He's not going anywhere."

"I still don't think it's a good idea," Eric grumbled.

"Yeah? Well, I don't think you have any right to tell

me what to do!" she exclaimed, trying to keep her voice down. "You don't even know me. And you made your feelings about me clear earlier."

A sudden panicked look crossed his face. A moment later, he smoothed his features back to pseudocalmness. "What are you talking about?"

"Back on the yacht. It's obvious you don't think I have any right being with Stephen since my bloodline's not as pure."

"I—what?" Eric looked truly startled. "No! No, that's not it at all. I didn't even know about that when we met."

"Sure," she said, crossing her arms over her chest. "Then why were you so surprised about our engagement?"

"Because . . . I mean, because you're so different. You saw him out there in the pool. You just don't seem like that type."

"What type? The fun type? Are you saying I'm boring?"

"No!" Eric wore the desperate look of someone trying to dig himself out of a hole, only to see the sides cave in. "You're so quiet and . . . serious. He's not."

"He has his moments. And I was out having fun too, you know. I had a drink. I danced." Her words came out in more of a defensive tone than she intended, probably because Stephen was also always telling her she didn't live it up enough. She really had been out there in the thick of the party, trying to share in his wild side just as he sometimes attempted her more decorous behavior. Stephen certainly excelled at making a spectacle of himself, but he did have a quieter side. "Just because I didn't make an idiot of myself doesn't mean I'm some kind of recluse."

"That's not what I—damn it!" Eric took a step toward her, frustration all over him. He raked a hand through his platinum hair. "This wasn't how I wanted this to be at all."

Her fury dimmed for a moment, turning to confusion. "What was it you wanted?"

"I—nothing, nothing. Forget it. Just be careful with Dennis. Go use a different feeder next time."

"Thanks for the advice I didn't ask for."

He sighed and seemed to be working hard to control his temper. "I'm just looking out for you, that's all."

His eyes suddenly lifted to something beyond her. Turning around, Rhea saw the brown-haired girl he'd been with earlier standing farther down the hall, watching them. Like Eric, she was dripping water everywhere. Her expression was hard to identify exactly, but Rhea felt pretty confident it wasn't happy.

"Hi, Emma," he said, looking like he wanted to be anywhere but in that hall right now.

"Hey," Emma replied stiffly. "I tried to find you, and someone said they saw you down here. Weren't you going to change clothes?"

"Yeah . . . I just ran into Rhea, and we started talking about Stephen's amazing dive."

Rhea arched an eyebrow and toyed with the idea of contradicting him. But the more she studied Emma, the more Rhea could now see that the other girl's expression was obvious jealousy. It was nothing Rhea wanted to get involved in, so she allowed him his lie.

Eric put on a big smile, catching Rhea by surprise. In their brief acquaintance, his few smiles had always been small or melancholy. But this . . . this smile went a long way to win Emma over, and even Rhea felt her breath catch a little.

"See you around," he told Rhea breezily. He walked past her and put an arm around Emma, leaning his face close to hers. "Now that you're here, maybe you can help me change after all."

Rhea repressed a grimace, but his remark erased the last signs of jealousy on Emma's face. She cuddled up against Eric and made some vague good-bye to Rhea. Rhea watched the two of them stroll off, whispering and laughing, and was surprised to feel a pang of sadness inside her chest.

Immediately she shook it off and decided she'd just go to bed. Why should she care what this Eric guy said or did? She'd barely exchanged a dozen words with him. Resolved, she started to head upstairs toward her room.

A moment later, she reconsidered and decided to tell Stephen good night.

Unsurprisingly, he was still outside, in the center of the party. He was soaked to the bone, and she wondered how many times he'd been in the lagoon. Vampires liked Chile in the winter because of the shorter sunlight, but the night was growing increasingly chilly. Liquor could only warm you up so much. Stephen didn't seem to notice the temperature and was telling some story about the time he and some friends had broken into their math teacher's office. The story involved vodka and ferrets.

Rhea smiled in spite of herself and waved at him as she emerged from the house. Catching sight of her, he gave her a big grin and put his story on hold.

"Hey, babe," he said, coming over to her. He reached out for a dripping hug.

She laughed. "No way."

He gave her an exaggerated sad face and then settled for a brief kiss on her lips, making sure to lean in far enough so she wouldn't get wet.

"Acceptable?" he asked triumphantly.

"Very. I just wanted you to know I'm heading to bed."

This time, his sad expression was real. "But we're going to set some shots on fire. You could help."

"That's not quite the use of my magic I had in mind. At least being so soaked, you probably don't have to worry about catching on fire yourself."

"That's true," he agreed, apparently thinking of it for the first time. His face softened slightly. "We'll talk tomorrow?"

"Yeah, of course."

Eric might think Stephen was just some loud, in-your-face guy, but Rhea had learned long ago that her fiancé possessed a fair amount of vulnerability that few ever saw. As far as she could tell, she was the only one he ever showed that side to. He seemed to take comfort from her, like he needed to express his softer side in order to balance that other rowdy part of him. They'd grown up around each other, almost like siblings, and the engagement had seemed perfectly natural. They were both used to having the other around.

He squeezed her hand—his was wet, naturally—and then gave her another quick kiss before returning to his audience.

Five

*E*mma was easy enough to soothe once Eric brought her back to his bedroom. She seemed much more interested in helping take his clothes off than discussing what had happened with Rhea, particularly since neither of them ended up putting on dry clothes or returning to the party.

Alcohol eventually made Emma fall into a heavy sleep, but as he lay in bed with her in his arms, he discovered he wasn't as lucky. The sounds of the party outside wound down. It was getting pretty late for the Moroi and he knew the dark-tinted windows would eventually be lightening, sending most of his friends to bed. He stared at the ceiling, growing more and more sober, thinking about Rhea Daniels.

And really, it made no sense. Aside from those first

few moments when they met, the two of them had yet to have a friendly conversation. Everything he said seemed to make her mad, and he couldn't figure out why. He knew he shouldn't worry about it. Who cared if she was touchy about everything? If she wanted to keep picking a fight, that was her problem. He'd have nothing to do with her.

And yet . . . no matter how often he told himself that, he still couldn't shake the image of her radiant hair or wise eyes. Who needed the sun if you were around her? In those first moments on the boat, when she'd truly seemed to get how he felt about his mother, he'd had a brief flash of someone really and sincerely understanding him. No, more than that. Someone who actually cared. Although her attentions hadn't been directed at him, he'd sensed that same characteristic in her when she'd spoken to the feeding room attendant and even that crazy Dennis guy. Rhea paid attention to people, to individuals.

He finally fell asleep, only to wake to a pounding headache. Emma, as always, displayed no symptoms of a hangover. She gave him a long, lingering kiss and tugged back on her still damp dress, promising to meet up with him in an hour to get blood before the next set of activities. They didn't know exactly what was going on, but Jared had promised something entertaining.

When Eric joined Emma, she had changed and was

as fresh and beautiful as ever, with no sign of her earlier disarrayed state. Eric had discovered his own shower had erased most of his headache, and linking hands with her, he allowed himself to relax and make an effort to enjoy the day.

The feeding area was much busier in the vampiric morning, since that was a preferred time to take blood. Eric and Emma stood in line, chatting with friends who looked like they'd done a bit too much partying. Someone came by with a stash of doughnuts pilfered from the breakfast buffet and passed the pastries out to the waiting group as appetizers to the blood.

When they reached the front of the line, Eric saw that a different attendant was on duty today. She marked their names on her list and waited for the next opening. When it came, she turned to Emma and said, "Go ahead, down to Dennis on the right."

Eric caught Emma's arm as she took a step forward. "Don't." He turned to the attendant. "We'll wait for the next one. Let someone else in line go."

The attendant started to protest—probably not liking someone dictating her job—but after a moment, she just shrugged and waved in the next person. Emma gave Eric a puzzled look, but another feeder became available before she could question him.

When they finished, she immediately jumped on the topic while walking back to the main part of the house.

"What was that about? The feeder thing? Why did you stop me?"

"Because that one's crazy," Eric replied.

"They're feeders," Emma said. "They're all crazy."

"Not like him. He was the one Rhea went to last night, and I would *not* want to be under the same roof as him if I were her. He was nuts. Total stalker obsessive type."

Emma pondered this and then shook her head. "Yeah, well, it's not like feeders are out socializing with us. She probably doesn't have to worry." There was a carefully calculated pause. "I'm kind of surprised *you're* so worried about her."

Eric recognized that tone and realized he'd stumbled into dangerous territory. "Not that worried. I hardly know her—but after talking to that guy last night, I would have warned anyone away from him."

"You were asking a lot of questions about her yesterday." Emma still apparently wasn't convinced of his lack of interest. He sighed, realizing he'd put Rhea on Emma's radar.

"All I asked was about Stephen being engaged. Come on, Em. Don't dig up something that doesn't even exist."

"Okay." She grinned and squeezed his hand, and he hoped the matter had truly been dropped. "Let's see what Jared has planned."

What Jared had planned was a scavenger hunt. Once

the guests (those who had been able to get out of bed) were gathered outside, their host explained the rules. Everyone would be divided into teams of two and be randomly given a clue. That clue would lead to another clue and so on until one of the teams found the ultimate treasure and won the game's prize: getting to stay in the beach house's master suite, complete with a Jacuzzi and balcony.

Emma gripped Eric so tightly that her nails dug into his skin, kind of reminding him of last night in bed. "We are *so* winning that," she hissed. "I just hope they don't send us all over into crazy places. Did you see those cliffs on the other side of the island? Molly claims Jared goes rock climbing all the time. No way am I doing that."

"And to make it more challenging," Jared announced, "we're going to randomly assign teams. Each person on the winning team gets one night in the suite."

This was met with a mix of cheers and groans. Emma was one of the groaners until Jared drew her name along with a friend of hers named Fiona. Emma lit up and kissed Eric on the cheek. "Okay. We've got this. You and me are gonna be in that Jacuzzi tonight." She scurried off to join Fiona.

Jared continued pulling out names from his hat, finally reaching, "Eric Dragomir."

In spite of his best efforts to ignore it, Eric couldn't help but notice the excited whispering among some of the gathered girls. They knew he and Emma weren't engaged yet, so some still considered him open game. Even a few guys looked interested in being paired with Eric, in the hopes of currying favor with his family.

Jared read the next name. "Rhea Daniels."

Eric froze.

He'd spotted Rhea as soon as he'd come outside earlier. She was standing with Stephen on the far side of the lagoon, seeming to be in a good mood. She and her fiancé had been having some kind of serious talk—not like a depressing talk, but just something warm and ordinary. Stephen had done most of the talking, his pleasant face earnest and thoughtful while she simply listened. The sun hadn't quite gone down yet, and its rays made her hair shine like gold fire. Eric couldn't look away from it and jealously wondered what they'd had to talk about.

Now, hearing her name, Rhea became puzzled and scanned the crowd. Stephen nudged her and pointed over at Eric. Her gaze fell on him, and her eyes widened in shock. For a moment, he was confused. If she was going to be shocked, it should have been when she heard their names called—not when she saw him. Then he understood. Rhea really didn't know who he was. He'd suspected it that night on the yacht but had thought that surely she'd have learned since then. Apparently not.

Stephen grinned and motioned for her to go over to Eric. Biting her lip, she reluctantly walked over, looking as though each step was agony. Glancing back to where Emma stood by Fiona, Eric thought his girlfriend looked as though each of Rhea's steps was agony for her, too.

Eric and Rhea said nothing to each other as more names were read off. They didn't even speak when they were given their clue. As the rest of the group eagerly dispersed, Eric looked down at their slip of paper.

Find me where the palm trees bend
By the water that never ends.

He stared at it blankly, having no idea what it meant. Rhea sighed and took the clue from him.

"It's a fountain," she said. "I saw it last night. There's a little path that goes out past the courtyard."

She marched away from him, and he hurried to keep up. Wordlessly she led him to the fountain. Delicate and made of marble, it was crowned with swans that poured water from their mouths. Eric couldn't decide if it was tacky or elegant. He and Rhea studied it for a while, trying to figure out what the next step was. Eric was the one who spotted it. A small piece of smooth, flat wood was embedded into a tiny gap in the sculpture. Words were engraved upon it.

Music, music everywhere
With sweeping sights that make you stare.

"The conservatory," said Rhea promptly. "It's on the upper floor."

Again, she took off, with Eric quickening his pace to stay with her. "Have you been here before? How do you know where everything is?"

"I went exploring last night," she explained tersely. It was clear she wasn't in the mood for conversation. At least not with him.

Sure enough, they reached the conservatory, which was filled with windows showing breathtaking views of the ocean. Another team was just leaving, uncertain if they'd read the clue correctly. Everyone's starting clue had sent them to a random place, and the goal was to eventually put them all together. The conservatory's clue was hidden on the piano. Like before, Rhea interpreted it and started to leave, but Eric grabbed her arm.

"Wait, I need to talk to you."

She raised an eyebrow. "Talk about what?"

He sighed. "Look, I just want to know why you're so mad at me today. What did I do this time? I already told you I wasn't making fun of you and Stephen last night."

Rhea studied him for several seconds, and he wondered if she'd just turn around and leave. Instead she answered his question with a question. "Why didn't you tell me you were a Dragomir?"

He hadn't expected that. "It . . . didn't seem important. And I thought you probably knew."

"Right. Because how could there be anyone in the world who doesn't know who you are?" she asked sarcastically.

"I'm serious! And I . . . well, I kind of liked you not knowing. You talked to me like a real person . . . even if it was to yell at me most of the time."

"I didn't yell," she countered. "And somehow, I don't believe you just wanted to talk to me. I've heard about you. You go through lots of girls. You probably thought I'd be an easy one, desperate to hook up with as much royalty as I can."

Eric gaped, wondering just what kind of reputation he had. It was true that he'd had a lot of girlfriends. But he'd never used them. He'd genuinely liked each of them, and he had intended to take his dad's advice and get serious, but then . . . well, Eric just always lost interest.

"That's not true at all! I like being with you because you're easy to talk to."

Rhea scoffed. "I thought you just said I yelled at you all the time."

"Well, that's not what I—I mean, that is, I like that you pay attention."

"Pay attention?" she asked warily.

"You notice things. You notice people—and you *get* people. You're the only one who thought about the massacre six months ago, you know. That's where my mother died."

She blanched, and all that annoyance and anger vanished. "Oh God, I'm sorry—"

He held up a hand. "I know you are. That's the thing. I've never met anyone who thinks about those things. You think about the servants. About that crazy feeder. I mean, don't get me wrong—a lot of these people are really nice. But there's something real about you. Something different. And that's why you're with Stephen, isn't it? I watched you guys earlier. You notice parts of him that no one else does, and he needs that. No one else cares about him that way." Eric paused, bracing himself for the next part. "But here's the thing, does anyone care about you? Who worries about you or asks how you feel?"

Rhea averted her eyes, which he thought was a damn shame. He could easily lose himself in them. "Plenty of people do," she said evasively. But he knew even she didn't believe that. She was quiet and went unnoticed, giving her energy to others and no doubt letting her parents urge her into a marriage that would save her from the disgrace they'd faced. Stephen, silly as he might seem, did care about her. That much was obvious. He was dependent on her to listen to what he was afraid to tell others. Eric doubted Stephen returned the favor.

"Not enough people do," Eric replied. "Somehow I just . . . know. I can see it all over you. You don't let people worry about you enough."

And then, doing what was probably one of the stupidest things ever, he pulled her to him and kissed her. He fully expected her to jerk away or maybe even punch or kick him. Instead she pressed closer, kissing him with an intensity that surpassed his own. He was the one who broke the kiss, suddenly conscious of their situation.

"Oh God," she breathed, face full of confusion. "I shouldn't have—I don't—"

"We should talk more," he said, wanting badly to kiss her again. What was happening to him? How had this situation spun out of control so quickly with someone he barely knew? "But not here. People will be coming through. Will you meet me later? Say at . . . eleven? Back by the fountain? The game'll be over."

"I don't know. . . ." But he could see in her eyes that she would.

"Eleven," he repeated.

At last, she nodded. Ecstatic, he kissed her one more time, wanting to leave on a high note. As he did, he heard a familiar voice call, "Hey, it's over here!"

He hastily pulled away, but it was too late. Emma stood in the doorway. A few moments later, a breathless Fiona joined her. Emma, Eric, and Rhea stood frozen and stunned. Fiona, who had missed the incident, looked confused.

Then, without a word, Emma turned and ran off. Eric's heart sank, and he remained motionless. It was Rhea—still always compassionate about others—who spurred him to action. She nudged him. "Go talk to her. She needs you. Forget the game."

He hesitated, not wanting to leave Rhea, but he knew she was right. Eric wasn't sure what was going on, what he felt for Rhea, but he owed Emma an explanation.

He hurried out of the room, past a still confused Fiona, just barely hearing her say to Rhea, "So, wait. Are we partners now?"

Emma had been fast. She was nowhere in sight, so he went to the most logical place he could think of: her room. He stood outside knocking for five minutes, but no answer came. She could have been ignoring him or simply hiding somewhere else.

Dejected, he returned to his room, unwilling to face anyone else. He spent the rest of the day lying on his bed, counting the minutes until eleven. Over and over, he thought about Emma and Rhea, coming to a final conclusion. He liked Emma a lot—but he didn't love her. He didn't love Rhea, either—but there was something about her that made him want to get to know her better, some electricity he felt in her presence. He couldn't shake the feeling that maybe she wasn't just another girl on his list.

Around ten, he made another attempt to find Emma—and failed. The game had long since ended, and everyone was too excited about it and that night's party to pay much attention to him. So he headed to the fountain to wait for Rhea, hoping to figure out at least one part of this mess. At eleven exactly, he sat on the ground next to the swans and waited.

And waited. And waited.

Almost an hour went by with no sign of her. Sad realization hit him. She'd changed her mind. Really, he should have expected it. She was engaged to someone else, and Eric was an idiot to interfere with that. Dejected and embarrassed, he finally returned to the house, where he found Stephen sitting by the pool and drinking with friends from their school.

Eric—figuring Rhea had told her fiancé all about being assaulted in the conservatory—expected Stephen to attack him. Instead the other guy offered a friendly smile. "You want to join us, Dragomir?"

Eric swallowed and shook his head. Rhea had apparently kept earlier events secret. "Nah, got stuff to do. Um, hey, have you seen Rhea? I just wanted to congratulate her on us failing miserably."

Stephen laughed. "Doesn't surprise me. But no, not sure where she went."

It didn't surprise him? Rhea was so smart. She could have won that game, and Stephen had no clue. Eric kept his thoughts to himself and went inside, asking around to find out where Rhea's room was. Someone gave him the location, and bracing himself for more rejection, he knocked on the door. The doorknob turned—but it wasn't Rhea.

It was her roommate, who said she hadn't seen Rhea since breakfast. An uneasy feeling bubbled up in Eric, though he didn't know why. Emma had disappeared too, but he wasn't worried about her. No doubt she was sequestered with friends. But Rhea? What about her?

He spent the rest of the night anxiously trying to get information about either girl and failing. The partying started up again, and he finally caught a glimpse of Emma in the crowd. She made eye contact and then pointedly ignored him. He let her be, glad he'd found one of them and that his instincts had been right. She was okay. Mad, but okay. Hating to bug Stephen again, Eric still forced himself to casually inquire about Rhea once more, saying he'd never caught up with her.

"She's around," Stephen replied easily. "Sometimes she just likes to be by herself. She'll turn up."

Eric wasn't so sure. His sense of worry was growing, and he wished he could convince Stephen to share in it. Eric finally decided he'd try Rhea's room one more time—but never got there. He was stopped when two guardians came charging out of the house.

"What's wrong?" he asked them. Panic flooded him.

"It's not—it's not Strigoi . . . ?" Eric couldn't face that again.

"Hardly," said one of the guys, sighing. He looked fierce like all guardians—but also annoyed. "We've got a runaway feeder. He can't get off the island, but with the way they are, he'll probably fall off a cliff and drown. Mr. Zeklos would never let us hear the end of it."

They pushed past Eric, leaving him wide eyed. Suddenly he knew where Rhea was.

Six

*R*hea wasn't sure how it had happened—probably because she'd been unconscious for most of it.

One minute she'd been leaving the feeding room, about to head down the hall and meet Eric at the fountain, even though she figured it would turn out to be the most idiotic thing she'd ever done. He probably wouldn't even show. The next minute she'd heard a commotion from inside the feeding room and a strangled cry of surprise. Then Dennis had burst out of the room, wild eyed, and everything had gone black.

She'd woken up—with a headache—inside what appeared to be a cave. It was rocky and cramped, the uncomfortable ground only adding to her discomfort. At first, she could hardly make out anything, and then an opening in the stony walls became clearer. She could see the twinkling of stars—and a dark shape blocking some of them out.

"Dennis?" she asked tentatively.

The feeder turned around, a grin lighting his face at seeing her awake.

"Rhea! I'm glad you're up. I didn't mean to hurt you, but we had to get you out, and I was afraid someone would hear you. Are you okay?" He reached for her, and she took a hasty step back.

"Fine . . . fine . . ." She tried to stay calm and not betray the racing of her heart. "What's going on? Why are we here?"

"I've freed us," he said. "It was so easy. I don't know why I didn't think of it before. They were all so busy."

Rhea tried to get a glimpse of what was outside the cave. More ocean and trees—but a different view than that of the Zeklos beach house. Recalling the cliffs on the other side of the island, she had a good idea of where they were.

"Dennis," she said gently, using the soothing tone she always did with him, "we need to go back. People will be worried."

He shook his head anxiously. "No, no. They're oppressing us. Keeping us apart. Now we can be free. We'll stay here for a while and then find a boat. We'll run off together. Just you and me."

Rhea's gut response was: *You're joking.* But the crazed look in his eyes told her he was dead serious.

"We can't. We can't live here. We can't live back on the mainland."

"I'll take care of us," he said. "It'll be easy. That's what the pretty brown-haired girl said."

"The pretty—never mind. Look, it won't work. We have to go back. Please."

Dennis was undaunted. "You can feed off me as much as you want. You don't have to worry about getting enough blood."

"That's . . . that's not the problem," she said.

"What is?" His enraptured tone suddenly took a dark turn. The abrupt change in his facial expression made her cringe. "Don't you want to be with me? Don't you like me?"

"Er, of course." Rhea was desperately assessing her options. Part of her wondered if she could just charge past him. Judging by how the entire entrance was filled with sky, she had the uneasy feeling they were dangerously close to a cliff's edge. "But I liked things the way they were. I . . . I thought you were happy." Maybe playing his game would get her out of this.

"We were being denied what we truly wanted. What we needed." He moved closer, and this time, she couldn't dodge. There simply wasn't enough room. "They only let you feed once a day."

"That's all I need." Her back hit the jagged wall. "It's fine."

"No. I know you want more. *I* want more. I want it now." He pushed his body against hers, wrapping his hands around her waist. She struggled against him, hating the way she touched him, but he was stronger. "Do it. Do it now. Drink."

He exposed his neck, and she just barely managed to shake her head. "No . . ."

"Do it!" he cried, his voice blasting her ears. His hands gripped her tighter, painfully so. "Drink!"

Terrified, Rhea consented, biting into his neck almost before she realized what she was doing. The blood tasted as sweet as ever, but she took no joy from it, not even when his hold on her loosened a little. Frantically, she wondered what she could do. What if she drank more than usual? What if she drank enough to incapacitate him? He might pass out. And yet . . . all the taboos and warnings came to her about feeding too much. She might accidentally kill him, turning herself into a Strigoi.

He took the choice from her. With astonishing self-control, he broke away, his face radiant. "That was . . . amazing . . . ," he breathed. He looked completely ecstatic—and dangerous. "See? I can give you everything you need. I'll take care of you, and—ah!"

Something hit him in the back. Or, rather, someone. Eric Dragomir had crept into the cave, moving so quietly that neither Rhea nor Dennis had noticed. Glaring furiously, Dennis turned around and lashed out at Eric, slamming the Moroi into the wall. Rhea screamed. She would have expected Dennis to be mellow from the bite, but if anything he seemed supercharged, invincible in his high.

Miraculously, Eric remained standing. He charged Dennis again, and the two became locked in a fierce hold that neither seemed to gain ground on. Each struggled to shove away the other or at least get a punch in. Every so often Eric would manage to push Dennis back, and then Dennis would push Eric forward. The problem was, Eric's back was at the cave opening. If he was pushed too far, he'd stumble onto the cliff's edge that Rhea suspected was right outside.

With as little exercise as they got, feeders didn't have much muscle. Nonetheless, that lack didn't seem to hinder Dennis, and he began to slowly press Eric toward the opening, one step at a time. Eric sweated, his teeth clenched as he tried to fight back. Neither were trained like guardians, and there was something very brutal and primitive about the fight.

At last Dennis managed to get Eric to the cave's entrance, and that was when Rhea knew she had to act. She just didn't know what to do. If she tried to hit Dennis, Eric might get pushed farther out. Still, there seemed to be no other options, and it would be better if she took action sooner rather than later.

Running forward, she kicked Dennis in the leg,

hoping to knock him off balance. She did, but not enough to make him fall. He shouldered her away but lost a few steps to Eric. If she could keep distracting Dennis, Eric might be able to make progress again. Only, everything she tried seemed useless. She didn't have the strength to really land any punches. She didn't really even know how to punch. Eric began moving closer to the edge once more.

Then she caught sight of a rock sitting in the corner, a little smaller than a bowling ball. Hoping she could knock Dennis out the way he'd done it to her, she hefted the stone up, struggling with its weight. She and Dennis were similar in height, and gathering all her strength, she swung out with the rock and smashed it against his head. He didn't collapse like she'd hoped, but he did completely let go of Eric and stagger forward, disoriented. In fact, Dennis was so addled and badly coordinated that he kept stumbling farther and farther forward—toward the cliff's edge.

Rhea screamed again. "Stop him!"

Eric reached for the man who had just been trying to kill him, face frantic. Dennis, realizing what was happening, reached out to try and grip Eric's hands, but he'd lost his footing. The cliff's edge began crumbling, bits of rock and dirt pouring over the edge. Dennis screamed, trying desperately to hold on to solid ground—but failing. He couldn't reach Eric or secure footing. Realizing he might go over if he stayed at the edge, Eric thrust himself back to the cave, taking Rhea inside with him, away from the danger. Dennis disappeared over the edge, still screaming—and then a few seconds later, there was silence.

Rhea buried her head against Eric's chest, surprised to find herself sobbing. "Hey, it's okay," he said, stroking her hair. "You're safe. You're okay."

It was eerily reminiscent of the night they'd met on the boat, when he'd comforted her there, too. Unbidden, she remembered his question from the conservatory, asking who was ever there to comfort her.

Lifting her head up, she saw that Eric's face was stricken. He was as shaken as she was but putting on a good show for her. "Are *you* okay?" she asked.

"I am now that you're safe," he said, though there was a haunted look in his pale green eyes, one Rhea suspected she shared. Rhea had never seen anyone die before. Dennis had terrified her. She'd wanted desperately to escape . . . but she hadn't wanted his death. Surely no one deserved to die like that. Swallowing, she focused on Eric again.

"How—what are you doing here?" she stuttered out.

"When I couldn't find you . . . I just kept asking and looking. No one knew anything. No one thought anything was wrong." The bitterness in his voice rang out. "Then the guardians said Dennis escaped, and I . . . I just knew. I knew he had you. The guardians were still sweeping the house and not finding anything, and I remembered Jared talking about how he went rock climbing here. I took a chance."

Distantly, Rhea recalled Dennis saying a "pretty brown-haired girl" had encouraged him to run off with Rhea. Rhea had a good idea who that girl was but decided not to bring it up just yet.

"Why didn't the guardians come here?" she asked instead.

"They didn't believe me. They thought he was too drugged to be dangerous. They figured he was just hiding somewhere on the grounds. Plus Stephen said you take walks by yourself all the time, so no one thought you and Dennis were connected."

Eric was still running his fingers through her hair, and it felt like the most perfect thing in the world. "You should have tried harder to convince them. You shouldn't have come alone," she argued. "With your family . . . if anything had happened to you . . . there'd be no more Dragomirs. . . ."

He still seemed shaken by what had happened but mustered a small smile. "It was worth the risk. I was too afraid there'd be no more Rhea."

She stared up at him, hardly daring to believe anyone would do that much for her. A strange, wondrous feeling rose in her chest, and this time, she was the one who kissed him. It seemed so strange to be kissing in a place where death had just occurred before their eyes, and yet . . . it also seemed right. They were alive. The kiss was alive.

She wanted to keep kissing him forever and had a feeling he would have been happy to do the same. There were too many things to worry about, though. Horrible things. They had to get back and report what had happened. They had to . . .

"Emma and Stephen," she murmured when she and Eric pulled apart. "What will we do?"

"We'll talk to them," said Eric. He hesitated. "If you . . . I mean, if you want to . . ."

She studied him, reminding herself that she barely knew him. What did she want? She and Stephen had been friends for a long time—almost like brother and sister. He loved her . . . but she wasn't in love with him. Until now, she'd thought it didn't matter, so long as she cared about him. Now she realized it did matter. Love had to be more than liking the other person. She didn't want to break his heart . . . but she also didn't want to regret taking this chance to be with someone who actually seemed to want to be with *her* and not just what she could do for him. Eric had been right about her always looking out for others. Now, for once, she would do what she wanted.

"We'll talk to them," she repeated.

He linked his hands in hers and led her out of the cave, steering her clear of the cliff's edge. She had a feeling it was less about safety and more about making sure she didn't catch a glimpse of Dennis's body. The way back down to the house actually had a well-worn trail, explaining why both Eric and Dennis had managed to reach this height.

Halfway down, Eric stopped and stared at her, an awestruck look in his eyes. "What is it?" she asked.

"Your hair. Even in moonlight . . . it looks like sunshine. I'd never have to go outside again if I was with you."

She tugged him forward. "I think you hit your head in your heroic struggles."

"You were the heroic one," Eric said, stepping around a rock bend. "Reminds me of the stories from Russia my grandmother used to tell me. You know any of them? Vasilisa the Brave?"

"Nope. My family's from Romania. Never heard of any Vasilisa." Looking up, Rhea stared up at the sky thoughtfully. "But I kind of like that name."

Bring Me
to Life

ALYSON NOËL

For the dead travel fast.—Bram Stoker, *Dracula*

One

$\mathcal{I}$ stop.

Despite the mobs of people jostling around me, ramming their bags into my back and mumbling obscenities under their breath, I remain firm, rooted in place. Taking a moment to survey the airport terminal—from the filthy tile floors that have traveled so far from their original shade of white they'll never return, to the depressing beige walls sporting garish black signs with yellow arrows pointing toward important destinations like the toilets and the line for taxis and buses. I readjust the strap on the small bag of art supplies I'm toting and wonder what happened to the rest of my group—if they somehow got lost, turned around, confused by the signs and headed the wrong way. I mean, I can't really be the only one who made it this far—*can I?*

The crowd continues to shift and move until it finally thins out and it's just me, and him—Monsieur Creepy Guy, with the plaid pants, weird shoes, and ill-fitting, gnarled blue sweater. Or, as I'm in England, make that *Sir* Creepy Guy. And since he's holding a sign that reads SUNDERLAND MANOR ART ACADEMY, I've pretty much pegged him as my ride.

I move toward him, doing my best to ignore the overly affectionate couple before me—the way they grope each other, gaze into each other's eyes, and kiss like it's their first—even though, unbeknownst to one of them, it could very well be their last. Painfully aware of that small, familiar knot of cynicism that now resides in my gut—the one I've named Jake after the person who put it there. Remembering how we used to be like that, grope like that, kiss like that, until Jake woke up one day and decided he'd rather grope and kiss my best friend, Tiffany.

"Sunderland Manor?" the Creepy Guy says in an accent so thick it takes me a moment to realize he's speaking English.

"Yeah, um, I mean, *yes*, that's me." I shake my head, not faring much better with the native tongue. "I'm a Sunderland Manor—uh—*student*." I nod.

"So, 'at's it?"

I glance around and shrug, unsure how to answer. Unsure how any self-respecting artist in the making would take the time to painstakingly piece together a portfolio, hoping to gain entry into the newest, most exclusive art academy for youths (as claimed by the brochure), only to either miss the flight or just bail completely. But then, maybe they didn't need it as much as me. Maybe their lives are Jake and Tiffany free.

I sweep my long, dark hair aside and switch my army green art bag to my other shoulder. Still remembering the look on Nina's face when I chose it over the one she bought for the trip. I mean, even though I promised my dad I'd do my best to accept her, the fact that she gave me a turquoise bag covered in pink hibiscus flowers pretty much proves she's not trying all that hard to accept *me*.

"Name, please?" he says, or actually, snaps; it sounded way more like a snap, like he's in a big hurry or something.

"Um, Danika." I nod. "Danika Kavanaugh?" I say it like a question, as though I'm looking to him to confirm my own name. I roll my eyes and shake my head. Nice to know I'm as big a dork in the UK as I was in the U.S.

He nods, checks the box next to my name, and barrels right out the double glass doors, just assuming I'll follow—which I do.

"Um, what about my bags?" I ask, my voice high-pitched, overeager, in the most pathetic, *please like me* kind of way. "They said they didn't make it—do you think they'll deliver them—or will we have to come back?"

He mumbles something over his shoulder, something that sounds like "Deliver 'em," but he's moving so quickly, I can't be too sure.

"So, do you know what happened to all the others?" I ask, my gaze fixed on the back of his head, the bald spot glinting like a bull's-eye and surrounded by a thatch of hair so red it's suspicious, like he dyes it or something. Doing my best to keep up with this skinny old guy, who moves awfully fast for someone of his advanced age, gasping and wheezing with the effort, I say, "I mean, aren't there supposed to be a few more of us?"

And just after I ask it, he stops so abruptly I bang right into him. Seriously, like straight into him. *So embarrassing.*

"'Fraid it's too late for 'em now, miss," he says, totally unfazed by the way my carry-on bag just nailed him in the back. Not missing a beat as he eases it off my shoulder and adds, "Not with the way the mist is rolling in like 'tis."

I squint. My eyes crinkled, nose scrunched, gazing all around and not quite getting what he means. Yes, it's a bit overcast, cloudy, and gray, but hey, it's England, that's pretty much a given, right? And the thing is, I don't see any fog. Not even a trace. So I turn to him and say just that, sure I misunderstood due to his accent and all.

But he just looks at me, gaze stern, fingers flapping at me to hurry up and get in. "Fog got nothing on the mist," he says. "Come along now, got to get moving before he gets any worse."

I huddle in the back of the van, pulling my navy peacoat tightly around me as he slams the door and settles in. Digging my fingers deep into the right-side pocket and fingering the small coin my grandmother stitched into the seam many years ago, back when it still belonged to my mom, long before she died and it was passed on to me. Squinting out the window, with my forehead pressed against the smudgy glass, thinking that if I just look hard enough I'll see this mist he's so worried about. But I don't. So I make one last attempt when I say, "Looks pretty clear to me—"

But he just grunts, hands gripping the wheel in the ten and two position, eyes on the road when he says, "That's how the mist works—'tis never what he seems."

I fall asleep.

I mean, it's not like I can remember the drive, so I guess that's what happened. All I know is that one minute we were pulling out of the municipal airport parking lot, and the next, it's like I'm in another world, jolted awake by a series of bumps in the road—a bad combination of really deep potholes and really bad shock absorbers.

"Is that it? Up ahead?" I squint into the distance, still unable to see any trace of that mist he's been mumbling about. Making out a large stone structure at the top of a hill that looks just like one of those creepy manors you read about in old gothic romance novels—the kind I like best. Like it's one of those drafty, foreboding homes filled with priceless antiques, hidden secrets, strange servants, resentful ghosts, and a lonely, plain-faced governess who can't help but fall for the tall, dark, and handsomely brooding master no matter how hard she fights it.

I reach over the seat and grab my bag, fumbling for my sketch pad, wanting to jot down my first impressions, document everything I see from beginning to end. But the road is too bumpy and my pencil gets dragged off the paper repeatedly, so I quit before I can really get started, and settle for gawking instead.

We pull up to a large, imposing gate, and the driver leans out the window, presses a button, and says, "She's here."

Which, frankly, I find a bit odd.

I mean, *She's here*? Shouldn't he have said, *We're here*? Aren't they expecting a group of us?

Five talented, lucky young artists chosen from a pool of thousands.

Five fortunate souls who not only aced a rigorous, multilayered application process but also had to submit a portfolio of paintings created specifically for this very event—a portfolio of paintings representing our dreams.

And I don't mean *dreams* as in *goals*. I mean the *nocturnal vision* kind. Since I've always had an active dream life, always had those kind of superpower, Technicolor, lucid dreams, the moment the brochure arrived in the mail I knew this was the school for me. Figuring I had a pretty good shot at making it, and it seems I was right.

But no matter how vibrant my dreams may be, I never dreamed of a place like this. A place with a drive so long and winding and steep, lined with lushly colored roses atop sharp, thorny stems that practically reach out and scrape the paint right off the side of the van. When we reach the top, I leap out and crane my neck all around, determined to take it all in.

Stone facade, gargoyles, flying buttresses, odd little carvings of winged creatures and gremlins—it's just . . . *spectacular*. Totally and completely *perfect*. It's everything I'd hoped for and more.

"Plenty of time for that later," the driver says, tossing my bag over his shoulder and heading for a door that's opened by a stern-faced woman, her long, gray hair coiled into a tightly braided spiral at the back of her head, dressed in a stark black dress with a white lace collar and apron to match. Her skin so pale and translucent, it's as though she's never known a single day in the sun.

"Now just look at ye. Ye must be Dani?"

I nod, wondering how she knew to call me by my nickname when I filled out all the forms as *Danika*.

"I'm Violet," she says, almost as an afterthought, as though she's too busy appraising me to pay attention to small pleasantries. "Well, you're a bright and pretty one, aren't ye?" She looks me over, her thin, dry lips curving up at the corners as the fragile skin around her eyes fans at the sides. "Young, strong, and made of good, healthy stock, I imagine. How old are ye?"

"Seventeen." I wrap my arms tightly around me, wondering if she's ever going to get around to inviting me in.

"Well, you'll do just fine here, ye will." She nods, ushering me inside and exchanging a look with the driver I can't quite interpret, adding, "Hurry on, now, you'll catch yer death out there," and leading me into a foyer so warm, so cozy, it feels just like home.

Well, not *my* home exactly. Not the overcrowded condo that used to be perfect back when it was just my dad and me—before Nina and all her "stuff" moved in—but the kind of home I *wish* I had. A house of mystery and history—filled with dark polished woods, antique rugs, large chandeliers, and bouquet after bouquet of those amazing red roses with long, thorny stems—pretty much the opposite of what I'm used to.

"Wow," I say, my voice barely a whisper as I gaze all

around, looking forward to exploring every nook of this place over the next few weeks. "This is just so . . . *grand*," I add, surprised by my use of the word. I mean, really? *Grand?* What happened to *awesome*, or *amazing*, or—

"Yes, 'tis comin' along, 'tis." Violet nods, yanking my coat off my shoulders, the chill of her touch lingering long after she hands it to the driver, who disappears with it upstairs. "Almost finished now."

I look at her, wondering what could possibly be left undone when it seems so finished, down to the last old-timey detail. Watching as she worries the odd, shiny, black pendant that hangs from her neck, her eyes raking over me as she points toward the ballroom and says, "That's where it started—the fire." She continues to scrutinize me. "As you can see, the restoration's not quite—*complete*."

I squint, gazing into a large room that really does bear a good deal of damage, and as I peer a little closer at the rest of the house, I see it's also showing a good deal of wear and tear I must've missed in my initial excitement.

"Come now," Violet says, her tiny, cold hand pressing against the small of my back. "I've made ye a nice supper and some tea before bed."

Bed?

I stop, my eyes seeking a window, but they're all covered by thick, heavy drapes. Wondering why she'd say such a thing when I know for a fact it's still light out—still morning, for that matter.

"Ye traveled a long way, ye did." She nods, as though she'd made the transatlantic journey sitting right alongside me. "Must be a bit jet-lagged, no?"

And just as I'm about to say no, that I'm not at all jet-lagged, that I'm completely wide awake and ready to explore until the other students arrive, she turns to me, watery blue eyes meeting mine as I hear myself say, "A bite would be good. I really am rather tired, come to think of it."

All that we see or seem is but a dream within a dream.—Edgar Allan Poe

Two

*J*t's cold. Frigid and bitter and cold. But it's not like I feel it, so it doesn't really affect me. All my awareness is focused on the insistent pounding of my heart as my feet cross the polished stone floor. Pushing through a mist so thick, so dense, it practically pulsates with life—as though it's a real, living thing.

It won't stop me, though. No matter how bad the visibility gets, I'll just keep moving forward, making my way toward that glowing red light. He's in here . . . somewhere . . . and he needs me to hurry. . . .

I flip the switch, squinting as the room fills with shadow and light. Noticing a thin layer of mist hovering all around, and wondering how it found its way in when the door is closed and the windows are covered with heavy, fringed drapes.

I toss my sheets aside and slip into the robe that was left at the foot of my bed. Pausing to run my fingers over the soft, silky feel of it, so different from the scruffy flannels I usually wear, and tying it snugly around my waist as I take in the large space before me—the dressing table covered with delicate lace doilies and silver-handled brushes and combs, the crystal chandelier hanging overhead, the stone hearth with embers still glowing from the fire Violet set, the small velvet settee just off to the side. And an easel that awaits me—all set up and ready to go with a fresh, new canvas just begging for me to bring it to life.

"Paint your dreams," I was told, and so I do. Wondering briefly if I should try to call home, let them know I've arrived, but just as quickly abandoning the idea. Now that Nina's moved in, my father's too busy for me, has probably forgotten all about me. Besides, I'd rather paint. I need to paint while the images are still fresh in my mind.

I retrieve my bag from the bench at the foot of my bed, glad I was smart enough not to check my very best brushes and paints along with the rest of my luggage. Squeezing color from the tubes marked black, white, and red, knowing that for this particular dream, a dream I've had before, but only in pieces, fragments, never as vibrant as this, it's the only palette required. And I'm so immersed in my subject, I hardly notice when Violet peeks in.

"Sorry fer disturbing ye, miss, but I heard ye moving

about and thought you might like somethin' to eat?"

She comes toward me, placing the tray on a small table beside the velvet settee, as I frown at my painting. I've been struggling with the mist for over an hour, and it still doesn't feel right. In my dream it felt so alive, but here, it's just a blotch of white static.

"I say, I'm no expert, but that seems to be coming along just fine, miss. Just fine indeed." She comes up alongside me and squints.

I shrug, twisting my lips to the side, wishing I could agree. Even though I've always been my worst critic—the fact is, it isn't quite there yet. Not even close.

"Maybe just a touch more . . . red. Right 'ere, miss." She points toward the center, the only place where any real color exists. "If ye don't mind me sayin' so."

I glance between her and the canvas, noticing how she looks so much younger than she did earlier—her face rounder, fuller, with a spot of color on each cheek. Blaming my earlier impression on a combination of dim lighting and jet lag, I focus back on my canvas and do as she says, then the two of us stand back to scrutinize it.

"As I said, I'm no expert, but it looks better now, doesn't it? Gives it a bit more . . . life—wouldn't ye say?" Her blue eyes light up as her cheeks flush bright pink, and for a moment she's so transformed I can't help but stare.

"It is better." I nod, glancing between her and the painting. "I thought I'd get dressed and head into town, have a look around and pick up some stuff to tide me over until my luggage arrives. Can you lend me a map or something? Or at least tell me where the shops are located?"

She bites down on her lip and narrows her eyes. And for a moment she seems upset by the question, but it's soon erased by her words when she says, "Sure, miss, I'd be happy to. But now's probably not the best time. Best to put it off for a while still, yes?"

I tilt my head, paintbrush dangling by my side, wondering what she meant by that.

"Well, in case you hadn't noticed, 'tis still dark out, and a long ways from morning." She heads for the window, drawing the drape in one quick move, showing a flash of pitch-black landscape before closing it again. "Oh, and you might want to watch yer paints there, miss." She points toward my feet. "A lot of work went into the restoration, and we'd hate to mess it up so quickly."

I lower my gaze, gasping when I see what looks like a pool of thick, red, viscous fluid swirling around me. But as soon as I blink, it's gone, and all I can see are the few small drops she promptly cleans.

"I'm sorry—I—" I shake my head, still stricken by what I know I saw just a second ago.

"No matter." She heads for the door. "Just—" She

pauses, eyes surveying me as she grasps the shiny black pendant hanging from her neck. "Just mind yerself, that's all."

The moment she's gone, I put my painting aside and decide to get dressed. I mean, even though it's the middle of the night, the fact is, I'm so wide awake now, I may as well do some exploring and check out the rest of the house. So after shivering under a weak spray of water that never really ventured anywhere past lukewarm, using some kind of weird, oddly scented, handmade soap that made me long for my nice, sudsy body wash back home, I sit at the dressing table, comb through my wet hair with one of those silver-plated combs, and dab on a little perfumed oil from an old-fashioned glass bottle, hoping to kill some of that soap stench. Then I go searching for the clothes I arrived in, since, thanks to the airline losing my bag, I have no other option.

But after checking the armoire, the chest of drawers, and just about anywhere else you could stash a black V-necked sweater, faded jeans, and a navy blue, hand-me-down peacoat, and coming up empty, I ring for Violet, only to be told they've been sent out for cleaning.

"But now I don't have anything to wear," I whine, realizing my voice has risen a few octaves louder than planned. But hey, I'm an only child, I'm not used to people messing with my stuff.

"Sorry, miss." She averts her gaze in a way that makes me feel this big. "Just trying to keep things runnin' smoothly."

I sigh. Knowing that to say anything further would just peg me as a spoiled American brat. Besides, wasn't the whole point of coming here to improve my art and experience something different from my suburban L.A. condo community? Not to mention, enjoy some time away from Jake, Tiffany, and Nina? And now that I'm here, maybe it's time I embrace it.

"Sorry." I shrug. "I didn't mean it like that—it's just—"

"I'll check on them come morning." She nods. "I'm sure they'll be returned to ye in good time. But for now, why not pick something from this here armoire to wear?" She smiles encouragingly. "There's some beautiful gowns in there, miss. Real antiques they is. It's all part of the restoration. Every last detail was noted and attended to."

I tilt my head and scrunch my nose, not near as convinced as she. I'm not really into fancy vintage gowns. I'm much more of a peacoat-and-cargo-pants girl.

And I'm just about to say it, just about to ask if she could possibly find something a little less fussy, when she says, "Don't really know which type ye are until you try a few, right?"

I squint, wondering if I voiced the thought out loud, though I'm pretty sure that I didn't.

"Besides," she adds, "it's not like you're goin' out or anyone's comin' in—at least not anytime soon. So if it's bein' seen that's got ye worried, forget it. Even though it's still dark out, I'm afraid the mist has rolled in so thick now, he won't be burnin' off fer days, maybe even a week. Everything's been delayed because of it, so you may as well enjoy the free time."

"But what about the other students?" I ask, wondering who I feel worse for, them or me? I mean, yeah, it's kind of cool to get a head start and poke around on my own, but a little artistically inclined company wouldn't hurt either.

"Oh, I'm afraid I don't know about that, miss. But I will say, they won't be coming by today, that's fer sure."

She heads for the armoire and removes a red silk gown with a deep plunging neckline, tight bodice, and full, trailing skirt. Gazing at it in such an admiring, covetous way, I'm about to suggest she wear it herself when she turns to me and says, "Didn't you ever play dress-up, miss? In your mum's clothes?"

I squint, thinking about my *mum*, a no-nonsense, no-frills, hardworking third-grade teacher who didn't really have many occasions to dress up for, or anything to really dress up in—unless you count cotton cardigans and pleated khakis, that is.

"No," I say. "Not really."

She looks at me, her eyes glinting with excitement. "Well then, I'd say now's as good a time as any."

Fools rush in where angels fear to tread.
—Alexander Pope

Three

"Now normally, I'd be slipping you into a corset and pulling the strings so tight you'd be screaming for mercy, but nowadays, you're all so skinny and muscled from athletics, a corset's no longer necessary, at least not in your case."

"Nowadays?" I turn to look at her, wondering if I need my eyes checked, as she appears even younger than she did a few minutes ago. Shaking my head as I gaze at the mirror, knowing I'm somewhere on the side of thin-*ish*, but not skinny. Definitely not skinny. Nor sporty, for that matter.

She bites her lip tighter and fastens the long row of tiny, covered buttons that line all the way up the back. Her fingers moving so quickly and nimbly, you'd think she did this sort of thing all the time. "So, what do you think?" She pushes me before the full-length mirror as she stands off to the side, just out of view.

I gasp, astonished by the way my normally way-pasty complexion is practically transformed, providing a lovely contrast to the deep, gorgeous red of the gown, and the way my chest practically heaves, appearing far more abundant than I know it to be, thanks to the ultra-low neckline. And as I run my hands over the severely nipped-in waist and soft folds of the extra-full, bustled skirt, I can't help but think how it suits me.

Even though I never thought of myself as *this* kind of girl—the shiny, fussy, sparkly kind—even though I've always preferred neutral colors and clean, simple lines, maybe I've had it all wrong. Maybe *this* is who I really am. And it took just one day at an art academy in England to discover it.

I turn from side to side, unable to stop mirror gazing. Wondering if it's possible to really start over, start fresh, and completely reinvent myself.

Wondering if it's possible to wipe away the memory of Jake and Tiffany and Nina, simply by discarding my old look for this dazzling new one.

I gaze at my hair, admiring the way it dries in soft, wavy tendrils that curl around my face, and the way my normally unremarkable brown eyes now seem to spar-kle with life. "I think—I think I'm looking at someone else!" I say, my fingers lost in the deep, silky folds of the skirt as a smile widens my pink, flushed cheeks.

"Maybe ye are?" Violet whispers, her gaze somber, far away, as though lost in another time and place. Then, shaking her head and returning to me, she adds, "But you're not through yet."

I cock my head, taking in my reflection and counting so many jewels, ribbons, and special effects, I'm wondering what we could possibly add that wouldn't send this dress straight over the top. Then I turn to see her heading for the dressing table and lifting the lid off a silver-plated jewelry box, retrieving a beautiful velvet choker with a gorgeous, shiny, black-beaded pendant hanging from its front that's very similar to the one she wears.

"It's made of jet," she says, answering the question in my gaze, as she fastens it around my neck. "The fossilized remains of decaying wood often found right here in these very cliffs." She nods, grabbing a few more pieces she secures in my hair before standing back to survey her handiwork. "The Queen often wore it as mourning jewelry."

"Mourning jewelry?" I raise my brow. "That seems a little . . . *grim*, doesn't it?"

But Violet either misses the comment or chooses to ignore it, because a moment later, she just claps her hands and says, "You're perfect, miss. Just *perfect.*"

The dress is gorgeous. Totally and completely gorgeous. And even though I decide to go with it, and all the jet jewelry Violet foisted on me, when it comes to the shoes, well, that's where I draw the line.

Never mind the fact that, just like the dress, they fit so perfectly we both gasp in astonishment. Never mind the fact that I can't help but feel just the tiniest bit Cinderella-like when I perch on the velvet settee and slip that elaborate velvet pump right onto my waiting foot. Because the fact is, there's something integral left out of that particular fairy tale: The truth about glass slippers is they don't make for comfortable footwear, and the same goes for these.

"But you *have* to wear them," she says, voice raised and urgent, eyes wide and fixed on mine.

Her gaze so convincing, so compelling, I'm just about to fold and give in, when I force myself to look away. Finding my voice again when I say, "You like 'em—you wear 'em." I shrug 'em off, replacing them with my trusty Doc Martens that fell under the bed. "Seriously, go ahead, knock yourself out. I'm sticking with these." I nod, clicking my heels together and smiling when the rubber soles make a dull thud as they bounce off each other.

She shakes her head and presses her lips so tightly together they're lined by a thin band of white, and I'm not quite sure how to take that. I mean, it's just a game of dress-up. What's the big deal? Why's she so invested in it?

"And yer breakfast, miss?" She pulls herself together, rubs her hands down the front of her apron, and motions toward the barely touched tray she'd left earlier. "Shall I take it?"

I gaze at it for a moment, about to let her have it, when I spot two of those delicious sausages I remember from the night before, and find myself overcome by a sudden craving for more.

"No, leave it," I say, my skirts swishing around me as I move toward it. Figuring I'll sit down and enjoy a quick bite before I set out to explore. "I'm actually pretty hungry," I add, already stabbing a sausage with my fork and enjoying the warm, savory flavor that explodes in my mouth as she quietly lets herself out.

Any relic of the dead is precious, if they were valued living.—Emily Brontë

Four

I'm surrounded by mist—thick, white, viscous mist. My hands held before me, cupped, as though I can scoop it out of my way. Only I can't. It slips right through my fingers and re-forms again. But no matter how indomitable it may be, it can't keep me from the glowing red light that leads me to him.

He needs me—and strangely, the closer I get, the more I realize I need him, too.

Just a few more steps and I'll be there—able to grab hold of the hand that's managed to pierce through the haze—grasping, reaching, beckoning for me to come closer—closer still—until—

At first it appears disembodied—obscured by the vapor—but the closer I get, the more I can see. A vague and shimmering outline of a tall, strong, darkly handsome *guy, with sleek black hair, straight nose, squared jaw, determined chin, high cheekbones, strong brow—but the eyes—the eyes are elusive, something I can't quite distinguish just yet—*

When I wake, it takes a moment for me to place it—the gown, the room, the tray of cold tea, untouched toast and eggs, and a half-eaten sausage lying diagonally across its plate. None of it making any immediate sense until it slowly starts to creep back—who I am, where I am, and why I'm dressed like this.

I raise my hands up high over my head and stretch from side to side. Amazed by how I could just fall asleep like that, right in the middle of eating, but then, that's what jet lag does—whacks out your body clock and throws you completely off balance.

But none of that's important, what matters is the dream. As I stand before my canvas, I'm amazed at how easily it flows, how these new images fit so perfectly into the scene I painted earlier. I'm just finishing up the last stroke of my subject's shiny, slicked-back hair when there's a knock at my door.

"Hey, Violet," I say, still focused on painting. "You can take the tray if you want. I guess I was more sleepy than hungry. I totally passed out."

"Great! Only problem is, I'm not Violet."

I turn to find a guy about my age leaning in the

doorway, his voice containing just the slightest hint of a British accent, one that's been heavily Americanized, when he says, "I'm Bram."

I lift a brow. Not really a name you hear all that often these days.

"My mom's a goth, what can I say?" He shrugs.

"And your dad? Is he a goth too?" I ask, taking in the dark, skinny jeans, the gray hoodie, and the black blazer he wears over it, thinking he looks so normal this apple must've fallen miles from that particular tree.

"My dad's dead." He nods, voicing it in a way I haven't been able to manage quite yet when it comes to my mom—totally neutral, without the slightest trace of quiver or tremble. Just a simple stating of the facts, with no room for emotion.

"I'm sorry." I place my brush on the ledge, then immediately regret it since I have no idea what to do with my hands.

"Don't be. I'm pretty sure it's not your fault." He shrugs, and when he smiles, his whole face lights up in a way that feels really familiar—or at least the parts I can see—the dimples, the straight teeth, the clear skin, but the rest is obscured by a pair of dark shades. "So, what's the deal around here? This is Sunderland Manor, right? Don't tell me I just broke into the wrong place."

I nod, still studying him closely, wondering if he's one of the missing students and really hoping he is.

"First good news I've had all day." He sighs, dropping his backpack onto the ground and making his way toward me. "First the airline lost my bag, then my train was delayed, and then I couldn't find a taxi to bring me here. Finally had to take three different buses and hoof it the rest of the way, oh, and I ripped my pants when I hopped the fence to get in. Not to mention this fog—what's up with this fog?"

"Mist," I say, my voice sounding ridiculously prim and proper, and wondering why I said it that way.

"Mist—fog—whatever." He drops onto the velvet settee, eyeballing the tray of food when he says, "You gonna eat that?"

"It's cold," I warn, coming around and perching on the chair to his right.

"Doesn't matter," he mumbles, already digging into what's left of the sausage. "I haven't eaten for—" He squints as though trying to calculate just when his last meal occurred, then quickly giving up and reaching for another bite.

"Didn't Violet offer to make you something?" I ask, remembering the warm welcome I received.

But he just looks at me, still chewing when he says, "Who?"

"You know, the house servant, or maid, or—whatever." I shrug, unused to living in a place where people actually wait on you, and unfamiliar with the appropriate terms. "She works here."

"All I know is no one picked me up at the station and no one answered the door. Took me forever to find this place, and I wasn't about to sleep on the porch, so I let myself in and went from room to room until I finally found you. Which, I gotta tell ya, is more than a little strange. I mean, where the heck is everyone? Aren't there supposed to be more of us? Teachers—students—and what about all those great-sounding classes they went on and on about in the brochure? From what I saw, there're no classrooms, no studio space—nothing even remotely resembling it. A little peculiar, don't you think?"

I watch as he finishes what's left of the sausage, my gaze lingering on the way his long, dark bangs fall across his forehead and land on his cheek. Strangely unbothered by anything he's just said, but knowing I need to reply in some way, I shrug and say, "Apparently there's been a mist delay." Absently picking at the folds of my dress, continuing to study him, I add, "So—what's it like? The house, I mean. I pretty much crashed just after I arrived, and I've yet to even leave this room." Cringing when I realize how I must sound to him—incredibly unadventurous, nothing like the real me, who would've fully investigated this place from the start. But for some reason, I just can't seem to summon that girl. Maybe it's the dress, the jet lag, or the sausage they keep feeding me, but the fact is, it feels so homey and comfortable right here in this room, I've had no desire to leave.

"Well—it's quiet," he says, wiping his mouth with a white linen napkin. "And appropriately creepy. My mom and her gang would totally love it." He tosses down the napkin and rises from his seat, turning toward me as he says, "Wanna go explore?"

"So, is this your thing?" He motions toward my dress, tracing the line between my head and my toes and back again, calculating, appraising, though not necessarily in a bad way.

I squint, having forgotten all about how odd I must look until he mentions it. Pressing my hands into the folds of the fabric, feeling inexplicably shy, and hoping he's not staring at the ridiculously low neckline, since I can't see his eyes behind his dark glasses.

"Oh, no—I—my bag got lost too—and they sent my clothes somewhere to be cleaned—so I had a choice between wearing a robe all day, running around naked, or raiding the closet—or the armoire, as the case may be—and, well, I chose this." I shrug, my cheeks heating as I quickly avert my gaze.

Not daring to look at him again until he says, "It's nice. Naked would also be nice." He laughs, the sound of it so oddly familiar, though I'm sure I've never met him before. "But trust me, I didn't mean anything by it. You look really pretty. If you ask me, more girls should dress like that. Though I guess it's probably not very comfortable."

"You'd be surprised," I say, remembering how I managed to fall asleep in it with no problem. "It's not so bad."

"Anyway, I think you'll find it's pretty hard to shock me. I just came here from a goth convention in Romania, Transylvania to be exact. My mom's band was headlining, and you can't even imagine the stuff I saw there."

"Your mom's in a band?"

"Yeah." He sighs and rubs his chin. "I try to be supportive and all, but—" He shakes his head and decides to let that one hang. "Anyway, I figured the dress was your thing. You know, art school, body as canvas and all that. Nice juxtaposition with the shoes, though."

I look at him, watching as he moves a few steps ahead, his black Converse sneakers making their way down the rug. And I can't help but compare him to Jake, who would never use a word like juxtaposition. Wouldn't even know what it meant.

"And the glasses—is that your thing?" I ask, my voice a mix of nervous flirtation and unadulterated geekiness, though unfortunately veering much more toward the latter.

"No. Not a thing, more like a necessity. I have issues with the light. I'm—sensitive." He glances over his shoulder at me.

"Oh, I didn't mean—," I start, feeling embarrassed for bringing it up.

But he just waves it away, waiting for me to catch up as he says, "Have you seen the library yet?"

I shake my head. "I haven't seen anything yet—well, aside from the dining room and my room, but that's about it," I say, entering a dark, wood-paneled room filled with comfortable-looking chairs, lots of reading lamps, a large stone hearth, and, of course, rows and rows of books.

"You a reader?" he asks, reaching for an old, leather-bound tome and flipping through the pages.

"Big-time." I nod, scanning the titles. "I especially like old gothic romances. I know that sounds weird, but I just have a thing for 'em."

"Then you'll like this one." He smiles, handing me a book with gold lettering on the front that spells *Dracula*. "It was written by my namesake."

"I've read it," I say, seeing the way he lifts his brow as he takes it from me and places it back on the shelf.

We continue exploring, checking out the dayroom, the sitting room, even an indoor swimming pool room I can't wait to visit later when my luggage arrives. Both of us stealing occasional glances at each other, eyebrows quirked, shoulders raised—both of us asking the same unspoken questions—where are all the classrooms, the teachers, not to mention the other students? Making a quick stop in the kitchen, where Bram goes straight for the stove, lifts a lid off a cast-iron pan, and grabs us each another sausage we munch on as we explore some more. The two of us ultimately stumbling upon the ballroom I glimpsed earlier, though just like Violet, it doesn't look near as aged, worn, and damaged as it did at first glance. In fact, even though there are still some visible traces of fire damage, it looks pretty good.

"This is where it started." Bram nods, head swiveling from side to side as he takes it all in. "According to the brochure, there was an out-of-control blaze that nearly burned this place to the ground. Look—" He points toward the walls, the ultrahigh ceilings, then traces his finger all the way down to the singed stone floors. "You can still see some of the damage. Weird." He shakes his head. "You'd think they would've fixed it by now."

"Maybe they want to remember." I shrug. "Or maybe they ran out of money and that's where we come in. As soon as this mist clears, all the other students will arrive and they'll hand us each a tool belt and tell us to get cracking." I turn toward Bram, hoping to make him laugh, or at the very least, smile.

But he just stands before me, head cocked to the side, taking me in as he says, "Too bad I left my bag in your room or I'd sketch you."

I look at him, wishing I could see his eyes so I'd know how he meant it. There's just something about him, something so . . . familiar—but then I quickly look away when he catches me staring.

"Really," he says, his voice soft, soothing. "The room, your dress, your shoes." He smiles. "It's just perfect. It really suits you. Maybe I should run up and get it?"

He turns to leave just as Violet comes in, takes one look at us, and turns white. And I mean white. Like just-seen-a-ghost white. Only there's no ghost, it's just us. And even though she quickly recovers, I can't quite forget the look that flashed in her eyes.

She moves toward us, her fingers nervously twisting at the hem of her apron, clearly not addressing me when she says, "Can I help you?"

"I'm Bram." He offers his hand. "One of the students."

"But you can't be," she says, her voice so quiet we both lean closer to hear it.

"'Scuse me?" Bram scrunches his brow and retracts his hand as he takes her in.

"The mist—we're invisible now—how did you find us?"

"Hard work, good luck, and a crap load of determination." He shrugs. "But—did you just say we're invisible now?"

Which is pretty much what I was gonna ask if he hadn't beat me to it.

But she just squints even further, so much that the

blue of her eyes is obliterated by a line of pale, sparse lashes and even paler skin. "Well then." She squares her shoulders and struggles to pull herself together. "I guess it's time we get ye settled in."

Despair has its own calms.—Bram Stoker, *Dracula*

Five

*T*he rest of the day is spent in my room, mostly working on my painting and trying not to think about Bram, which only leads to more thinking about Bram. I mean, *yes*, he's really cute. *Yes*, we share the same interests. *Yes*, he knows how to use multisyllabic words correctly in a sentence. *Yes*, he said he wanted to sketch me, which in my mind is pretty much the most romantic thing a person can ever say or do. But still, as cool as he may be, as familiar as he may feel, I'm also well aware, *painfully* aware, that I'm exhibiting all the telltale signs of a classic rebound situation.

Not that I've ever had an opportunity to have a classic rebound situation until now, with Jake being my first boyfriend and all. But after watching my dad go through it not long after losing my mom, when he just turned his back on the past and jumped right back into the dating pool with Nina, I'm pretty much an expert on these things.

Which is exactly why I can't indulge myself now.

Exactly why I need to look upon Bram as a fellow art student and nothing more.

And that's why I stay in my room. Determined to do what I came here to do, which is paint—*not* flirt, or hook up, or get emotionally attached to someone who'll probably just end up breaking my heart at the soonest opportunity anyway. And when Violet comes in to leave a new tray of food, including a plate of those sausages I like, I don't even ask if she's seen him, or what he's up to. I just carry on with my painting, as though Bram doesn't exist, until the jet lag kicks in, I fall asleep again, and the dream picks up right where it left off, with me fighting through the mist, grasping for his hand, only this time, his icy cold fingers entwine with mine, pulling me closer, begging me to see him, *really* see him, as a pulsating red glow emanates from his chest. . . .

And when I awaken, I head straight for my canvas and capture that, too, the long, cool fingers, the red glow, and am just making out the arch of his brow when a pale, blond girl comes in to clear the tray, takes one look at me, and suggests I change for dinner.

I squint, wondering where she might've come from, since this is the first I've seen of her. I wasn't even aware there was another shift of servants working here. Then I follow her gaze to my dress, horrified to see that I've ruined it, smeared it with paint, and wonder why no one ever offered me a smock to wear over it. I mean seriously, no teachers, no smocks, no designated art studio—what kind of art academy is this?

I take a deep breath and look up at the girl again, my mind suddenly flooding with a long list of questions. Questions that vanish the moment she returns my gaze and says, "Not to worry." Her voice is calm, soothing, eager to put me at ease. "I'm certain the dress can be cleaned, and if not, there's plenty more where that came from." She turns toward the canvas, her eyes growing wide as she takes in my progress. "I say, you've come a very long way in just a day's time." She clucks her tongue as her hands twist at her apron. "Such great progress indeed," she adds, her voice lifting. "Oh, and in case ye were wonderin', the instructors have also been delayed. But the good news is, this mist should lift in no more than a day or two now, and when it does, all will git back to normal again."

"Really?" I look at her. "Violet said it would be at least a week."

She looks at me, gaze thoughtful when she says, "Did she? Well, let's just say that things are lookin' up, miss." She tilts her head and looks me over, and something about her gaze, her movements, the way she clutches at her apron is so familiar. Then I realize what it is—she looks and acts like a much younger version of Violet, and I wonder if they're somehow related. "I'm Camellia." She nods, heading for the armoire. "Violet's me mum." She pushes through the row of dresses, choosing two and then turning toward me. "So, what do ye say, miss—the green or the purple?" She lifts a pale blond brow that's so light in color it practically fades into her skin. "They're both beautiful—both perfect for yer colorin'—couldn't go wrong if ye tried." She nods, dangling a gorgeous silk gown in each hand.

I glance between them, finding them both equally stunning, equally outdated, and equally alluring. Wondering for a moment what happened to my bag—the one full of cargo pants, jeans, and black sweaters, then meeting her gaze and dismissing the thought just as quickly.

Deciding to enjoy this new version of me for as long as it lasts, I say, "What the heck, let's go with the purple this time."

When I walk into the dining room, I almost don't recognize him.

No, scratch that. Because the truth is, I *do* recognize him—just not as Bram.

For a split second, when I find him at the table with his hair slicked back, and his modern-day clothes replaced with 1800s Victorian wear, he looks just like the guy in my dreams—the one who beckons to me.

I freeze. My breath freezes, my heart freezes, my entire body freezes, but then, when he turns and smiles in that familiar, easygoing way that he has, all systems are go again.

He's *not* the guy from my dream. He *can't* be. For one thing, he's here right in front of me. And for another, that just doesn't make any sense.

"Let me guess, they hid your clothes too?" I take the place across from him, the one set with fine china, crystal goblets, and more rows of silverware than I know what to do with. My eyes graze over him, taking in the white ruffled shirt, the blue waistcoat, and of course those glasses, which in an odd, unexpected way really seem to go with his clothing.

"No." He smiles, helping himself to so many sausage links I hope he'll leave some for me. "I found these in the armoire and thought I'd dress up to match you— you know, so you wouldn't feel so alone. What do you think?"

I look at him, allowing myself a quick glance, which is all it takes to make my stomach start to dance. Then I help myself to what's left of the sausage, grab my knife and fork, and dig in. "You look—nice," I mumble, between bites. "Proper, elegant"—*and sexy, and hot, and totally and completely irresistible*—"and, with the glasses, a little bit edgy, even," I stammer.

He laughs, dabbing his lips with the corner of his napkin as he says, "And you, fair lady, look stunning. That purple really suits you."

I press my lips together and gaze down at my plate, reminding myself of my vow to not get overly excited by his compliments.

"So, I see you're a fan of the sausage?" He looks at me, jaw dropping in horror when he realizes what he just said. "O-*kay*, not quite how I meant it, but, still, there it is." He shakes his head and laughs, heaping a generous lump of mashed potatoes and some unidentifiable boiled, limp, green thing onto his plate. "Can't say I blame you, though, it's good stuff. Wonder what they put in it?"

I shrug, covering my mouth as I say, "It's like hot dogs. Best not to ask."

"Ever try blood sausage?" He looks at me, head tilted as a smile plays at his lips.

I blanch, making all manner of grossed-out faces when I say, "Gawd, no, why would I? I mean, is it really made from *blood*?"

"Really and truly." He nods. "Pig's blood. *Usually*. It's good stuff, though. Don't knock it till you try it."

I stab a green bean and lift it to my mouth, inspecting it as I say, "Uh, no thanks, why would I even go there?"

He shrugs. "Well, one could also ask, why *wouldn't*

you go there? I mean, you're an artist, right?"

I shrug and pick at my food.

"Okay, so maybe you're not Picasso—*yet*, but you've got an artist's way of looking at things, which is nothing like the normal way of looking at things. Painters like you and me—we don't see life the same way as everyone else. We notice the details, all the things they miss. Then we add and subtract and interpret them in our own way. So, with that in mind, why would we ever choose *not* to try something? To just settle for the same ole, same ole? Why would you even consider signing up for the usual, mundane experience?" He leans toward me, his brow lifted high over the rim of his glasses. "And, as artists, it's practically our duty to look upon our lives as one long artistic experiment. The more you allow yourself to experience, the more your craft can grow. And trying new things is a very big part of that. You'll be amazed at how it feeds your imagination and frees your—*soul*."

I shrug, watching as he pours some red liquid from a decanter into my goblet, thinking, *Great. Now he thinks I'm an uptight prude!* And immediately chasing it with, *Who cares what he thinks? He's a fellow student, not a Jake replacement.* Clinking my glass against his and nearly choking when I bring it to my lips and discover it doesn't just look like wine, but it really *is* wine.

He looks at me, laughing when he sees my reaction,

then continues to drink and eat like he's used to dining like this.

"You actually like it?" I ask, watching as he makes good progress toward emptying his glass.

Seeing him nod when he says, "I've spent a lot of time on the road, traveling all over Europe with my mom and her band. It's not at all like the States, here there are a lot fewer restrictions. You can drink, go to clubs, live like an adult, it's all good." He smiles. "Everything in moderation—*right*? Or at least, *almost* everything."

I nod, immediately pegging him as way out of my league. I mean, a guy like that, a guy so worldly and experienced, would never be interested in a small-time girl like me. Not that I care or anything. I'm just saying.

"Your life sounds so . . . *exotic*," I mumble, finally able to look at him again.

But he just shrugs. "To me it's just—*my life*. It's what's familiar—what I'm used to." He spears a sausage link and chews thoughtfully. "The idea of going to a normal American high school—now *that's* exotic."

"You don't go to school?" I look at him, wondering how he qualified for the program, since it was open only to high school seniors.

"Nope, I have a tutor. Think of it like a traveling home school, if you will." He shrugs, running his tongue over his teeth. "My mom's been dragging me back and forth from London to New York since I was a little kid.

She yanked me out of public school way back in kinder-garten, didn't even let me graduate with my class." He laughs. "So how is high school? Is it anything like you see on TV?"

I gaze down at my plate, thinking about the hell I went through last semester when the whole humiliating Jake and Tiffany story broke. How everyone stared at me, gossiped about me, and how the couple in question obviously enjoyed flaunting it, by the way they always chose to make out right in front of her locker, which was just two rows from mine. I had no one to turn to. I was completely alone. My dad was too busy, Nina too . . . *bitchy*, and, unfortunately, for the last few years I'd relied so much on Tiffany, I'd forgotten to make other friends. And even though my coming here to England has han-dled the *out of sight* part of it, I'm still waiting for the *out of mind* part to follow. I wish it would hurry.

"It's nothing like you see on TV," I say, trying to peer into his glasses, see what lurks behind those dark lenses, but the only eyes I see are my own reflecting right back at me. "Nothing like it at all." I sigh. "Trust me, it's far worse than that."

The second we finish eating, Camellia clears our plates and tries to get us to head back to our rooms so we can paint. But we don't want to head back to our rooms, and our saying as much really upsets her.

"It's not like we need babysitting," Bram says, smiling at her in that charming way that he has. "If you want to head out—head out! We can look after ourselves."

She glances between us, obviously so unhappy by our refusal to go along with her plans I'm about to agree just to please her, figuring we can always just sneak out later. But when she disappears with a tall stack of dishes, Bram leans toward me and says, "What's *her* deal?"

I shrug. I don't know what anyone's deal is. I'm nothing like him. I didn't grow up on the road, drinking wine in exotic locales, with a goth band mom. I'm a half-orphaned only child, from an L.A. suburb, who's used to a pretty normal, ho-hum existence, who, oh yeah, just happens to have artistic ambitions. But still, no matter how weird it is here, with our clothes, the mist, Violet, and Camellia—I'm not the least bit homesick. I mean, yeah, I miss my dad—or at least the old version of him. But I don't miss Nina, or high school, or either one of my two former friends.

And the next thing I know Bram is beside me, offering his hand as he says, "Come on, let's ditch this place before she comes back."

We slip out the front door and straight into the mist, the two of us laughing as we stumble along, clutching at each other so as not to get lost. And even though his hand feels so good with the way his soft, cool palm presses tightly, and the way his fingers entwine so nicely with mine, I'm quick to remind myself that it's purely for practical purposes. So that we don't get separated and lose each other in the haze. No matter how nice, no matter how *right* it may feel, it means nothing to him, so it shouldn't mean something to me.

We move forward, slowly, carefully, heading toward the area where the mist is at its thickest, not realizing we've stumbled into a graveyard until I've fallen head-first over a tombstone.

"Must be the family plot," Bram says, voice coming from somewhere just above me as he helps me to stand. "And watch out for the roses. They're so big and vicious they practically jump out at you."

But a second after he says it, it's too late. I've already been scratched by one of those thorns, digging into the side of my neck, somewhere between my ear and the hollow.

I let go of his hand so I can assess the damage, my fingers slipping through something warm and wet that can only be blood—my blood.

"Too late," I say, wincing when I touch it again. "Maybe we should head back inside so I can clean it up, get a Band-Aid or something. Okay? *Bram?*"

I reach out beside me, in front of me, behind me, my hands groping into thin air, the space he just filled—but he's gone. No longer there. No longer—*anywhere.*

I turn all around, calling his name, as my arms flail

through the mist. But I can't see him. Can't see anything. And no matter how loudly I call, no matter how
many times I shout out his name, there's no response.

I'm alone.

And yet—*I'm not.*

There's someone else. Some*thing* else. And when I see
that soft red glow in the distance, I turn and run the
opposite way. Falling over a mound of freshly dug dirt,
not realizing until a hand is clamped over my mouth
that that loud, piercing scream came from me.

A wounded deer leaps highest.—Emily Dickinson

Six

hen he pulls me toward him, pulls me tightly to his chest, the mist clears. Everything clears. And at last I can see him, look right into his deep, dark eyes. His gaze probing, penetrating, luring me in, framed by lashes so thick they hardly seem real.

"You've come," he whispers, the words like a song on his lips. "You've come to save me, haven't you? You've traveled all this way, across oceans, across time, so that we can be together again." His dark eyes search my face. "Through so many years, so many lives, I've tried to find you, and I've finally succeeded. You're as beautiful as you ever were, as you've ever been. Look at me, please look at me and see me as you once did."

So I do. I gaze into his eyes and see all of it—everything. Our love, our grand, sweeping love, and the fire that *destroyed it in an instant . . .*

I press my hand to his cold, smooth cheek, shivering from the chill of his touch as he covers it with his own. "I'll make you whole again," I promise. "We'll live together, forever. We'll never be apart. . . ."

When my eyes meet his, I know exactly what I must do. And even though I don't want to leave, would do anything to remain here in this beautiful ballroom, wrapped in his arms, with the chill of his lips at my ear, my cheek, my neck . . . I must go. In order to have this forever—I must wake up and paint.

It's the only way. . . .

I open my eyes to a mist-filled room. Despite the fact that the doors and windows are closed, it snakes all around me—curling around my legs, my torso, my head, lingering at the stinging, wet sore on my neck as I rise from my bed and head for my canvas, knowing I must complete the portrait, finish the scene, then head downstairs and wait.

There is music. Soft, lilting music that drifts from below. Music that calls to me—signaling the time has now come.

The painting is done.

I place my brush on the ledge and stand back to survey my work. It's perfect. He's perfect. Just like my dream. And now there's only one thing left to do in order for my perfect lover to return to me.

One small task to make this restoration complete.

I gaze into the mirror and run my hands down the front of my black watered-silk gown with the deep, plunging neck. Having no memory of when I swapped out the purple one, but still more than pleased with the reflection that stares back. And when I see the way the mist curls and slithers around me, I know that he is pleased too. I understand now what I failed to see before.

He causes the mist.

He *is* the mist.

They are one and the same.

He leads me down the hall, the mist trailing behind me, in front of me, all around me, drawing me to the very end, where I stop before a large portrait of me— Lily Earnshaw—painted in 1896 and wearing the same gown and jewels I wear now.

I reach toward it, trailing my fingers along the smooth silk of the dress, the pale expanse of skin, feeling the sensation of my fingers as though touching myself, and knowing we are connected.

Art is life. Life is art. It's never been truer than at this very moment.

Moving to the one just beside it—the one of him. The frame is singed from the fire, its plaque missing, but I'm not the least bit surprised to find the portrait itself fully restored—just as he shall be, as soon as I reach him.

I head down the stairs and into the ballroom that's now fully refurbished—looking just like it does in my painting. The walls creamy and glistening and dotted with gold leaf, the floors shined and polished to their former splendor, as Camellia and some red-haired guy I assume is her boyfriend laugh joyously, heads thrown back, faces radiant, as they waltz across the room.

He waits in the corner—so dark and handsome, I can't help but rush toward him. Wincing as the chill of his touch sends an icy jolt straight through to my bones, as he presses my body tightly to his. The red glow that emanates from his chest drawing me closer, luring me near, begging for me to complete him.

My fingers slip through his dark, glossy hair as I bring his lips to my neck, closing my eyes against the feel of his tongue washing over my wound, as the excited, hushed voices of Camellia and her friend urge me to hurry, to get it done with already.

"We've waited so long for this moment," Camellia murmurs as her friend stands alongside her. "And it was well worth the wait, 'twas. Yer just perfect, miss, just like ye were back then. We knew it from the moment we lured you back here with the contest. Oh, do hurry up and kiss him already! You're the key! All yer dreamin' and paintin'—just yer presence alone was enough to spur the restoration in ways we could only hope for. And now it's time to complete it, miss, to restore Master Lucian so we can serve this house as we used to. Just one kiss, miss— 'tis all it takes—"

I turn. Did she say I was the *key*?

"Well, surely you realize by now that yer wearin' yer own dress and yer own jewels, and even staying in the manor that was always meant to be yers?" She shakes her head and clucks her tongue. "There was a bit of a mix-up—a misunderstanding of sorts—and then with the fire—" She twists the pendant at her neck. "But never ye mind that, miss—we can have it all again—start over, as it were—all you need to do is kiss Master Lucian, and the past is forgotten."

"Hurry up now!" her boyfriend says, his beady eyes narrowing on mine. "We's all been waiting a very long time—"

I turn toward him, Lucian, standing silent and still, unable to do anything more than wait patiently for me to begin. My blood dripping from his lips, luring me to press mine against them. Knowing that's all it takes, all that's required, one deep kiss and I can bring him to life.

He groans, grasping me tighter, so tight I can't breathe. His mouth moving against mine, at first softly, then with greater urgency, attempting to part my lips just ever so slightly—

And I'm just about to do it, just about to surrender, when I hear a muffled scream, a commotion, and I turn to find Bram standing behind me.

"Hey, Dani." He pushes his filthy, smudged glasses up past his forehead and onto his mud-slicked hair. "I hate to kill the moment you got goin' here, but trust me—you might want to rethink it."

I glance between him and Lucian, struck by their resemblance—the clothes, the hair, even their dark, heavily lashed eyes—everything identical, except for the way mist flows from Lucian's mouth, and words flow from Bram's.

"Trust me," he says, moving closer. "This is one guy you do not want to play tonsil hockey with. Remember when we got separated outside? That was no accident—that was them." He jabs his thumb over his shoulder toward Camellia and her friend, who cower behind him. "Oh, and that sore on your neck? Not a rose, like you think. I've yet to see the thorn that can do that particular brand of damage, leaving two strategically placed puncture wounds right smack-dab in the sweet spot." He shakes his head as he plucks mud, leaves, and debris from his shirt. "And as for that graveyard outside? That would be lover boy's most recent address. Seriously, he's spent the last century six feet deep, just waiting for you to show up and save him. And once he moved out, he tried to make me move in." He gazes down at himself. "Sorry for the mess, but I was forced to dig my way out."

"But that's ridiculous," I say, aware of Lucian's hands

on my back, my neck, urging me to turn away from Bram and back to him.

"I know it sounds crazy." Bram shrugs. "And believe me, I've got plenty more where that came from. But here's the thing, I've attended enough goth festivals through the years to know the real from the fake. And Dani, this ain't fake."

Lucian's hands are at my waist, while his lips push at my ear, and I know he wants me to kiss him again, more fully this time, while we still can. And even though I want to, even though I know that he's fading, just barely hanging on—I can't. Not when Bram's looking at me like that. Not when Camellia's freaking out. Not when there's still so much left unsaid.

"Did you check out your painting in the hall?" Bram shakes his head. "Is that creepy or what? But here's the thing. It wasn't painted in 1896, that's just what they want you to think. It was probably painted sometime last week."

"How would you know?" I say, thinking how ridiculous it is that out of all the things he's told me, that's the one I choose to question. But when I remember how touching the painting felt like touching myself, I narrow my gaze even further.

He shrugs, deciding not to push it when he says, "Anyway, I digress, that's hardly the point."

"So what is the point?" I lift my shoulder to my ear,

so Lucian will quit lapping at my neck.

"The point is, none of this is what you think. They're using you. You're their missing link. Your whole reason for being here is to paint the dead guy, raise the dead guy, kiss the dead guy, and bring him to life. Oh, and in case you haven't noticed, those two"—he points toward Camellia and her friend—"they're indentured servants, bound to the house. They live and die with it. It's a package deal."

And when I look at them again, I know that it's true. Camellia isn't Violet's daughter—they're one and the same. And the red-haired guy is the driver, the creepy old man who brought me here.

"Different flower, same girl." Bram shrugs, reading my expression. "Seems you and your paintings have restored them all."

"But—how?" I squint, confused by just about everything he's said. None of it makes the slightest bit of sense.

He looks at me, face composed and serious when he says, "They lured you here for the restoration. Trust me, Dani, this is no art school—or at least not the kind you were hoping for. There was never any real contest, no other students delayed by the mist—no other students at all! It's just one big, carefully orchestrated ruse to get to you. It was always about you, Dani. They needed your dreams, your vision, your talent—it's your artistic gifts that completed the restoration, returned everything back to its former glory. But as for your connection to the place—the way it feels so familiar—so homey—or in your case, even better than home, perhaps?" He quirks a brow and takes me in. "That's their influence. It's not real." He pauses, allowing enough time for the words to sink in. "You don't have to do this, you don't have to do their bidding. You're the one in charge here. All of this, everything you see, including them"—he motions toward the servants behind him—"depends entirely on you, and your willingness to go along with their plan."

And he's just barely finished when Camellia/Violet runs up behind him, gazing deep into my eyes when she says, "Don't ruin this for us—please! We only want what's best for the house—that's all we've ever wanted. And look! Look how beautiful 'tis again! You belong here, Lily—this is your home, and we live to serve you and Master Lucian!"

I glance from her to Lucian, the guy from my dreams. He needs me.

He's tremulous, faint, unable to speak. Neither alive nor dead—trapped in some kind of limbo state.

I'm sure of only one thing: This is my duty, my reason for being. My connection to this place is real, of that I've no doubt. I've never felt so at home, so content, so happy just to stay within these old walls. Besides, it's like Bram said, they're depending on me.

Hearing Bram's voice at my ear, whispering urgently,

"Listen, Dani, I get that you're wrestling with some issues at home, really, I do. But still, you don't really strike me as the suicidal type. But hey, if I'm wrong, don't mind me, just go ahead and kiss him already, that should do the trick."

I glance over my shoulder, annoyed by his constant interruptions and eager to get on with my destiny.

"Even though he appears animated—or at the very least, upright and visible—in order for him to be truly alive, he needs your soul. And to get it, he'll kiss you, suck it right out of you, extract the life force, and then spit out what remains so he won't have the burden of all that goes with it. Leaving you no more than an empty shell, which he may or may not send home in a box so your poor dad can bury you. Seriously, Dani, it's not just the stuff of horror movies—in this case it's real. See that red glow emanating from his chest? That's the void he needs to fill. Is that what you want? To be a soul donor for him?"

I swallow hard and turn back toward the guy from my dreams, the guy I came here to help, promised to help. But when I glance over my shoulder at Bram, a real live, flesh-and-blood person who's only trying to help me—save me from doing something risky that may not end well—that's when I choose.

Hearing Camellia's agonized scream crying out from behind me, as I push away from Lucian and rush straight toward Bram.

His arms circle around me as his mouth presses against mine—the feel of his lips so familiar, my mind floods with memories stretching far before my time.

Moving across my face to my cheek before working his way to the space below my ear, brushing my hair to the side, and he whispers, "This is forever," as his fangs sink into my flesh.

We loved with a love that was more than love.

—Edgar Allan Poe

Seven

hen I wake, Bram's leaning over me, all cleaned up with a new set of clothes and freshly washed hair, gazing at me with loving concern when he says, "Sorry, Lily. I didn't mean to surprise you like that."

"My name's not Lily," I mumble, struggling to sit up, though I'm far too weak to even lift my head.

"Well, it used to be." He smiles, running his finger down the length of my cheek. "But if you prefer, I'll call you Dani—or even something else entirely. We've got an eternity to get it all figured out, no need to rush into anything."

I look at him, gazing into eyes that look just like Lucian's, wondering how I got it so wrong.

Realizing my thoughts are no longer private, haven't

been all along, when he says, "You didn't. You didn't *get* it wrong, or *choose* wrong. The fact is, Lily-Dani, you chose the exact same way you did before. Over a hundred years ago. And apparently Lucian never got over it." He shakes his head. "Though I guarantee you he's over it now. I'm afraid my brother won't be visiting anytime soon."

"Your brother," I whisper as my hand flies to my throat, wondering which is more horrifying—the two sets of puncture marks, or the fact that I'm no longer breathing.

"Listen." He climbs onto the divan and grasps my hand in his. "The only thing I lied about was your connection to this place." He pauses, eyes gazing into mine when he adds, "Well, that and the painting. I painted it, over a hundred years ago, and you painted the one of me just beside it, but everything else was true."

"How could I have possibly painted that when I'm only seventeen?" I cry, his words not making the least bit of sense, even though deep down inside, I know them to be true.

"I've waited a long time to find you," he says. "Gave up on that reincarnation crap years ago. But then, when I heard about the restoration, I swung by to see for myself, and the moment I saw you, I *knew*. And when I saw your Doc Martens, I knew for sure. You always had that independent, rebellious streak, and well, you know the rest."

"But I don't," I say, my voice hoarse, scratchy, as though I haven't used it all day. "I don't know anything. All I know is that I'm no longer breathing, I think I might've killed someone who was already dead, and—" I close my eyes, unwilling to voice the worst of it, so I think it instead: *And I think I might be a vampire.*

"You *are* a vampire." He nods, and by the glint in his deep, dark eyes, it's clear he's quite pleased by the fact.

And was I a vampire before—a hundred years ago?

He shakes his head. "No. Although Lucian tried to trick you into letting him *turn* you, when you discovered it was he, not me, who tried to sire you, you fled. And in your haste, knocked over a candelabrum, which burned down the house and took Lucian right along with it. By the time I returned, there was nothing left to save. You were gone, Lucian was six feet under, and though the servants clung to the hope that he'd someday hasten your return, I never believed it. But don't worry about them—they bear no further allegiance to Lucian. Now that they know we've no plans to leave, they'll happily serve us for the rest of eternity."

I stare at the wall, the furniture, the heavy drapes that are forever drawn. Trying to make sense of it all, but it's a lot to absorb.

"Everything you see here is ours, just as it was always meant to be. You're an integral part of this house— without you, without our eternal love, it can't thrive, it all falls apart. It's been that way from the moment you first set foot in this place—over a century ago. The house was in a shambles but your mere presence was enough to start the process, and your artistic gift brought it to life. And that's when I knew you were the one I'd been waiting for. Your connection to this place is very real—this is where you are meant be." He looks at me, his gaze filled with reverence, voice soft and tender, when he adds, "I've waited so many years for you to return, Lily-Dani, and while Lucian may have sent you the dreams, it was you and I who were lovers. He met you first and swore that I stole you from him—but you can't steal what was always meant to be yours, now, can you?" He smiles, smoothing my hair between his thumb and index finger. "I know you remember. I felt it in your kiss."

"So what does it mean?" I ask, my gaze fixed on those deliciously chilled lips and longing to taste them again.

He smiles, exposing a full set of teeth, including, yes, fangs, kissing the tip of my nose when he says, "It means you'll live forever. You'll be young and beautiful forever. And you'll never have to deal with Nina, high school, or the likes of Jake and Tiffany again."

"And my dad? What about him?" I ask, suddenly overcome with the pain of missing him—a pain that subsides the moment I realize the truth: The person I miss is long gone. My old dad, the man he used to be, disappeared the moment he hooked up with Nina. Leaving behind a new, not at all improved dad in his place. One who barely takes notice of me. One who's clearly eager to forget the past and embrace a future I prefer to avoid.

He shrugs. "That's the only downside. You can never see him again. But still, there's always something, right? Nothing ever comes without a price." He slips his arm behind me, supporting my back as he helps me to sit. "But for now, you need your strength. You need to eat."

He rings a bell and Violet, still transformed into her younger self, Camellia, hurries in. "Miss." She bows before me, no longer wielding any type of strange power over me. No longer daring to make eye contact now that our positions as mistress and servant have been newly established. Setting down a plate piled high with sausage links, she says, "They're fresh. Courtesy of that nice young stable boy from the next manor over."

Bram glances between us, then dismisses Camellia with a wave of his hand. "So." He leans toward me. "More of that blood sausage you seem to like so much?" He smiles. "Or—more of *me*?" He loosens his collar, exposing an area of his neck I vaguely remember feeding from—just after he bit me.

And when I look at him, I know it's just one more experience I need to embrace—one that won't just feed my art, but also free my soul—like he said.

I glance at the mirror before us, seeing him with his slicked-back hair, black waistcoat, black pants, and white frilly shirt, and me in my black watered-silk gown, with a jet-black tiara now secured at my crown.

And I reach for him, pulling him to me as my lips swell toward his. Remembering how it felt to be loved, truly loved, all those years ago, back when we first met, and knowing I've found that love once again, I lower my head, press my lips to his neck, and drink.

Aware of his arms circling around me, lovingly, protectively, bringing me home.

My real home.

The one that was always meant to be.

Above

KRISTIN CAST

One

*E*arth.
She sits in her belly, swallowed by dirt,
   desolate
   bruised
   broken.
Part of the world no one desires, entombed among creatures that slime and bloat with waste.
   She is a tree root stuck below:
           suffocating,
                    twisting to break
                                 free.
Whispers from those that surround her tell
"you are safe
held in a warm embrace
Below."

She is a virgin of safety. Always intimidated, attacked, tormented.

No air. No light. No possibility or wonder, joy, love, protection.

Home

she has not found you.

But Above . . .

The thought tickles her heart and makes her tan skin melt, sticky and warm. Her daydreams float images of happiness Above.

Above, she can be alive.

Above, she can be safe.

Anywhere is better than Below.

From her perch Below, she stares up. Her hair, the color of fallen leaves in dry season, falls down the back of her fur garment. Her neck muscles tight with dreaming. A crack in the hollow earth glistens with heat of a setting sun. Its width and length greatly reveals the blue Above and the possibility of looking upon

the Others.

She waits, searching for a glimpse.

Shaking with anticipation, excitement, her body sips shallow, noiseless breaths. If she reached up, her fingertips could play peekaboo with the floor of Above.

There! An Other! Heading to shelter, its home in the trees, as its sun fades. Its sweet smell drips through the cracks of her cocoon. Shattering fear.

They, the Others, are high-reaching and jointless. Their skin, barely covered by the hides of their kills, the dark of wet earth. She matches them, the Others. She too is dark skinned. Not the shiny brightness of stars like the ones Below; their pupils large, sucking light from the nothing.

She is unique, evolved, brave.

Her difference, the seed of abuse.

She touches, sees, hears, smells, tastes, wants . . . different.

Alone in a pit of ancestors who have forever grown Below. Who have forever grown afraid of the light and the Others Above, created strong and deadly, who survive by it.

She has been exposed to sixteen years of fear and hate, warned of the murdering Others that stalk Above, waiting to suck out bones of those Below who are captured. Their skin sacks left to ooze and twitch on mounds together, eyes left open to watch the flies hatch families of their own.

Still, she is forever in awe of the openness that is Above.

Sitting, staring, waiting, she dreams of an escape from Below, from her torturers who eat at her soul like grubs. A new life, name, family, home. To touch the

sun's warmth and drink the moon's calm rays.
To love and be free.
To love and be wanted.
To love and be avenged.

Two

"Hey, girl." A putrid voice hurled toward her. Ten spidery fingers wet with acid spit reached up, picked at her loose dress, and skittered up and down her bare legs. "Come down here and join us. We got some nice toys for you to play with." The one who spoke licked the blade of his knife while others snapped their belts and threatened her with tight fists.

Male laughter fought through her ears and set off her stomach. Bile churned, threatened to surge past her teeth and coat her body in sick. She rocked back and forth, silently chanting a spell of fading protection.

Ten fingers still touching.

I will be okay.

Stomach still falling.

I will be okay.

Bodies still threatening . . . *I will be okay* . . . taunting . . . *I will be okay* . . . waiting.

She was "punished" for being different. It was "fun."

I will be okay.

Above.

Above.

Above.

"Don'tcha wanna see what we got waitin'?"

Lick. Snap. Pound.

No, go away, go away. "I'm fine up here."

"Aw, come on. It'll be fun."

Lick. Snap. Pound.

Help! Go away! Help me! "No thank you. I'm fine."

"Whoo, boys! Ain't she cute, so proper."

More spiders bit at her legs, filling her with poison. Daring her stomach.

"Rheena!" Her birth mother paused the girl's hell. "Oh, hello, boys. Shouldn't y'all be gettin' ready?" Rheena unpinched her eyes, stomach relaxing. "Well then, pick up your jaws and get goin'." They smirked hexes toward the girl and were gone.

For now.

"Ugh. You need to learn to stop distractin' them from their duties. *Whore.*"

With one arm she ripped Rheena down from her seat of dreams and let her topple to the mud below.

"It is almost time for the kill. We must prepare them to go. *Above.*" She thrust one glowing shoulder toward the heavens, scrunching with fear and disgust; the last word a whisper. Her celestine blue eyes flicked, aware of the commotion around them. The hunters gathering their killing tools. Rheena could not see into the dark that engulfed them. "Come, girl. Wipe yourself off, you're always so filthy. I'll never get why you sit up there near the sun and risk bein' seen by one of them Others." Again, a whisper. As if speaking their name would tag those Below for death. Rheena smiled inside, hoping so. "It's morbid, Rheena. Revoltin'." She followed her birth mother's rant, dancing around pale bodies that shuffled about heavy and quiet with angst, until the opening of their cave was reached.

"Umm, excuse me?"

A sigh hissed past her birth mother's lips as she turned toward Rheena. "What is it now?"

"Could I go Above, with the men? Just once?"

"You are such a stupid, stupid girl."

Rheena was made to stand outside the mouth of their dwelling, invited in only when her father could be bothered with the sight of her. She nervously watched glowing figures buzz in and out of the openings of their hivelike residence. *Don't leave me alone. Out here. With them.*

"Do we really have to do this shit every single month?" The familiar speech from her birth father could be heard booming from outside their den where Rheena waited.

Always waiting.

"You women do not go *Above*, especially to hunt. It's men's work. Part of bein' a man. Why does that girl keep havin' to ask? She's gotta know that my answer's gonna be the same. No!" He paused, but as with all of the men Below he did not expect or want his wife's response. "Now bring her in here and I'll tell her. *Again*." The creak of his large wooden chair signaled that he had sat, exhausted and repulsed by the girl waiting outside. Like the months and years before, she tensed, waiting for her birth mother to shove her back inside to be greeted by her father's mask of hate and disgust.

But this time, something changed.

Rheena's birth mother cleared her throat; her voice shook with hesitation. "Should we actually stop her this time?" No answer. "I mean, she desires the Above so bad she will probably kill herself just tryin' to go up there. Shouldn't you just let her go?" The birth mother hurried along, allowing, hoping for no interruption. "No one'll ever pick her to breed, and she can't see good enough to even do simple tasks that need to be done around a house and for a man. We'll be stuck with her and everyone'll always look at you and me like we're no better than them that never grow. Really, you have done everything you can for that girl. So, I'm gonna ask again, should you stop her?"

"No."

One word decided fate.

One word proved love.

One word: free.

Her birth mother, the inventor of Rheena's new end, tore out of their cave, wrenched the girl's arm from her side, dragged her down a musty corridor, and thrust her into a large hole beneath the earth. With hateful satisfaction, her birth mother left the glowing inhabitants of the massive area firm instruction: "She is to go Above with your men as they hunt. She is not to return." Rheena received nothing from the woman as she left.

Surrounded by hunters.

Surrounded by fear.

They waited for the final curve of the sun to set. There was no threat from the Others when night rose. The towering creatures were unable to survive in the absence of their sun. For stepping into the moon's time, the dark, awakened the Reaper.

The men Below began their ascent herded together.

The mass grew hot with testosterone and killing fantasies. Rheena was groped, pushed, tripped forward as they marched

        up

    up

up

out of their hole.

Ants.

Three

*C*risp air still sprinkled with sun swirled around the girl birthed from the earth. Hunters scattered as she stood, motionless and thankful.

At last.

Inexperienced and young, she had no plan.

Only hope.

Always hope.

"Rheena." Her earth name floated, kissing the sky, murmuring good-byes. *Home. Have I found you?*

Light from the rising moon rubbed the dark of her hair. It shone onyx appreciation. The nameless looked around. Her old tribe shot arrows of annoyance and hate into her alien figure. They knew she did not join them for the hunt. The care she used when maneuvering through the thick grasses made their anger boil. *How could she respect the Above?* The grass tangled her new limbs, threatening to pull her back to where she was filthy stupid fun. She looked up as they looked out. She stood with arms outstretched as they crouched in hiding, waiting.

Always waiting.

They sank deeper into the tall grass, camouflage. Neglecting her Above as they had Below.

Except one. A man's ten spidery fingers wet with acid wove silent promises into her soul.

I will hunt you.

Find you.

Kill you. Lick you dry.

Freak.

Four

She separated, nameless. Her cord cut.
Alive.

A broken spirit, she gently toured the mossy forest floor wide eyed, happy. She greeted the trees with her palms and poured her bare feet over their roots. She could feel the remnants of heat left by the summer sun and thanked the skies for their breeze.

The hunters were still close. She had not yet escaped the proud, primal outbursts of the kill. A wounded animal's cry shattered through new friends' trunks. It frightened her bruised body and flipped her down on the crunch of leaves.

The fall
      soft. Deceptive.
What sat in wait under,

betrayal. Always waiting.

An Other's trap of rope had sprung. The nameless girl hurled back. Her friend's rough, thick frame proved unforgiving. Black spotted before her eyes, wordless beetles.

Five

The sun awoke and knocked on Sol's open window. Without its presence his sleep was a coma. It tickled his neck and danced in song on his bare ebony chest.

Wake up, sleepyhead.

> *Do not go straight back to bed.*
> *It's time to rise! It's time to shine!*
> *It's time to open your trap and dine!*

Music, passion. Wove jingles from nothing.

Open your trap and dine? "That is correct. I should have one from Below waiting."

Waiting?

Captured, hooked, snagged.

> Hostage.

> Murderer.

The Other wrung his mantis fingers, cracked his giraffe neck in preparation.

Ritualistic.

His kill. His feelings. His movements. All planned. Forever the same.

Murderer.

Sol opened the front door, calm.

Murderer.

Eyes closed, arms opening to embrace the scream that would engulf him. Part of his present.

Murderer.

But nothing. His gift echoed no noise.

Murderer.

"Nothing?" Sol deflated. Eyes cracked open. "Wait."

A something.

He robotically approached.

"What are you?"

The rope and leaves released, spilling the nameless. A young woman. Wrong color skin. He yearned for cloud white.

Wrong. All wrong.

Birdlike, he twitched fascination, curiosity. No emotion, never any.

She is unseen, alone, new.

He carried her inside. Placed her in his bed.

Effortless power. Strength of the gods. Speed stolen from wind.

Was this act compassion?

No. Never any.

This was wonder. Emotionless.

Six

With the sun awake, watching, he stayed hidden beneath dead leaves, dead bark, dead dirt.

Separated from the other hunters. There could be no witnesses.

Coward.

"Whore thinks she can run away and we'll just forget about her. Fucking freak." Psychotic laughter fell off worm-wet lips and wrapped around the knife. His knife. "No, no, no. We weren't done playin'. I say when it's over, an' it ain't over yet." He slept with the stink, waiting for the moon.

Killer. Coward.

The torture tool whispered, sadistic. Craving. Happy. *Kill her.*

We will kill.
Bleed her.
Bleed her, taste her, lick her dry.
She asked for it. For us to kill.
Born a freak.
Kill kill kill kill killkillkillkillkillkillkillkillkillkillkill-killkillkillkill. Yummmmm.

Seven

The girl awoke to touchable sounds.

And sun.

Thick vibrations twisted in its heat, comforting waves uncovered consciousness, washed over her body, healing, empowering.

Black pulled back from her eyes, revealing alien surroundings. She sat up. No words could roll from her mouth. A mind sinking heavy and blank. The music that had pulled her back to life ceased. Allowing pain to drill holes, invade from skull to spine. She winced, teeth grinding, reality fading, sleep racing to catch her. It was interrupted, cut off by deep molasses.

"You are safe here."

Emotionless wonder.

Safe. You, girl, nameless, unwanted, abused,

discarded. Are safe.

She turned to him, corking pain. Every beat of her heart matched a blink of his eyes, eggs dipped in emerald mystery, suspended in a face smooth and unlined. Below could be consumed, wither in those eyes.

Sol nodded and continued to play.

Music. But this was different from the harsh beats from Below.

This was passion.

The Other's smooth black frame melted into the female-shaped string instrument, becoming fluid. Ink plucked off the pages he played from, constructed as man.

His music choked her insides.

Reshaping.

Making new.

Tears pricked her eyes, jumped from her chin, slid through her neck. Seen by the sun. Nude. New. Exposed.

His song ended and his eyes toured the wet face. *Innocent, beautiful.*

Beautiful. You, girl, nameless, unwanted, abused, discarded. Are beautiful.

"I have upset you?"

Pause

only the leaves rustled in reply.

"You need not be frightened. I will do you no harm. You are too . . . changed."

Emotionless wonder.

The girl blinked slowly, pushing doubt from her eyes. He was next to her. *An Other.*

Five feet took only a moment.

Cold blew from his smooth frame. Sewed chills through her arms.

"Well, I should be afraid, but . . ."

I am too changed?

"But I'm not."

Pain from the journey upward, to protection, sprang active. Her head burned hot, angry.

Eyes closed

                 she coiled her legs to her chest.

Sinking again

                 into opaque sleep.

Sol caught the nameless new girl, kept her from crashing.

A mistake?

Their species was not destined to feel without murder. Not designed for natural emotion.

With her touch he now felt all.

      Sucked hurt and burn from her body

              filtered through him

                   leaving shadows of emotion.

Green crystal eyes shook with her pain

             her wants

               her needs.

Let go!

She is unique.
The Other looked at her
              alone
              unsure
              beautiful.
Not knowing what happened.
Wanting more.
              Wonder fled.
              Desire consumed.

Eight

he had felt the connection.

Her life, a puzzle.

Pieces hidden.

One found.

The Other blinked, stood. Again empty of emotion.

Rational.

"I am Sol."

He wanted her touch. Not her words.

"Oh, umm . . ."

Peeling her eyes from his,

she searched for a new identity,

not wanting to be tied to the harshness of her given name.

"Aurora. I am Aurora."

She pointed toward her chest as if forcing the name

within her heart. A cool, sun-scented breeze played with the ripe auburn of her tangled hair as she looked around the small room. Her eyes lifted to the windows, and she could see that she was no longer near the earth. Aurora jutted her neck forward and rushed past Sol to the line of windows opposite her.

Her body tense with excitement and wonder.

"How did I get here?"

Her dangerous journey to his place in the trees had warped memories.

"I caught you. You were unconscious, so I brought you in here and waited with you."

Rational.

Emotion?

Never. Not any.

Except

with her touch.

"You caught me?"

She turned to him. Her positivity turning to annoyance and fear. Pictures of her past becoming clear.

Could this be the end?

No. She had felt something. *They* had felt something. A beginning.

She believed what he had said. She was safe. There. With him.

And

she was *too changed*.

Aurora let her question, her doubt slide out her ears
                              down her shoulders
out the window.

She wanted nothing to get in the way of what she was
feeling.

Finally feeling.

Finally trusting.

Finally happy.

But still, curiosity lingered.

She crossed the room. Back to him.

"Tell me why you kill. I want to understand."

Nine

He had listened to her words, but could only focus on her lips.

They had barely moved

yet said so much.

Sol wanted to press his close to hers and feel. Block out words and let bodies rush together.

He let his fantasies mellow before speaking.

"Come with me."

He led her deep into his home and gestured for her to sit at a table covered in papers. Musical dots and tails flicked across the pages.

He took a seat across from her.

"The people you are from, their bodies are luminescent, their pupils consume and reach out for light. That light that courses through them gives us something here, Above.

Something that we must drain.

Something that we must drink."

His lips parted. A row of teeth revealed. All the same.

He pushed his eyelids together.

Wait.

Two, different.

He had released his canines. Carved to points. Sharp. Deadly.

And gone.

"I do it for this. My music. What you heard, what awakened you, I cannot create

alone.

Without your people, their brilliance

I cannot imagine.

I, *we* are absent

of feeling, touching.

Of having

true emotion."

Sol fluttered his fingers toward her, daring himself to touch.

"I do not need it to live;

I need it to be alive.

But you, Aurora, you are extraordinary."

Her heart crept toward her throat. She wanted to pull him to her and sob thank-yous into his chest.

Am I home?

"Your touch can fill me with the same life I would have had to kill for."

Aurora knew she should, but could not be disgusted by him and could not fear him. She had felt the same hooded emotions in her cell Below.

Those are not my people now. They never were.

Without thinking, she slid her hand on his. It was cool stone beneath her fingers.

His eyes began to roll back and he closed them, inhaling.

"What do you feel?" Aurora whispered.

Sol smiled and opened his eyes. Aurora sat before him, waiting for approval.

"Everything."

She is beauty.

Sol reached across the narrow table and led her face to his.

Warm lips touched, pressed. Exchanged new feelings.

Warm lips pressed, parted. Connecting secrets.

He had circled the table without leaving her and now tucked her body within his. He kissed her deeper and felt his fangs jut out.

He pulled his mouth from hers.

His first time

embarrassed.

Aurora smiled and slid her finger back and forth across the points of his teeth. "It's okay."

She accepted him, wanted him completely.

No more waiting.

She pulled him back to her.

Music, *his* music, fell through her body.

Desire loosened her hands as she fumbled with buttons, zippers, ties. She had never wanted, never meant, never felt so much.

Love, home, she has found you.

Ten

ight awoke and stirred sleeping promises. Moonlight crept into the hidden two.

   Killer. Coward.

Wake.

You must wake.

We must hunt.

The man sprang up. Fueled by the decay of his bed and sick, sweet pictures of a blood-covered girl.

   Killer. Coward.

He scraped his drool onto the knife, charging it for its upcoming task.

Find her.

Killer her. The freak. The whore.

We must kill.

Now now now now nownownownownownownownow-

nownownownow. GO!!!!!!!

He skittered across the floor of Above. She would be easy to find. He knew her voice. He knew her smell. He knew she was close.

Eleven

Sol lay next to beauty, love. Staring into her as she spoke of her past, her dreams, hopes, wants, needs, love.

Not touching.

Still feeling.

She had changed him.

He had emotion without her touch. Within her, he had found himself.

Twelve

"*O*f course, the first thing she's gonna go do is hook up with one o' them Others and be some murderer's slut. But he can't protect you now, no sir. He can't protect you at all."

His deranged rants were heard and answered:

You must teach her.

She needs to learn a lesson.

Bleed her, taste her, lick her dry.

She asked for it. For us to kill.

He slithered up up up. Tearing clothes, scraping flesh. Unaware of pain. His knife calm, waiting nestled between wet teeth.

Killer. Coward.

He had reached her. Rough bark stuck to his hands, sweaty with desire, anticipation. Night cloaked him, but he still stood in shadow, drinking in the moments before he was realized by his prey.

She asked for it.

Kill her.

He released the blade from his mouth and painted his lips with its excess spit.

Kill her.

His breath quickened, revealing his presence. She quickly turned and his body began to tingle.

"Let's see what's under that blanket, girl."

Before she could scream, run, fight, feel, process, he was on her. She landed with a *thwack* on the wooden porch. Her blanket torn open as he sat on her twisting bare stomach. Four spider fingers fought past her teeth and pinned her tongue.

"Shh, shh, shh, don't cry. It's gonna be fun."

Thirteen

Sol awoke to find the space next to him empty and the sun silent.

Every room.

Vacant, alone.

But the front door

open.

"Aurora? Are you out there?"

New feeling flooded.

Panic, misery, denial, anguish tore from his stomach, splashed at his feet, and bought Sol to his hands and knees.

"Nononononononono." Whispers.

He crawled to her.

Innocent, beautiful.

Her mouth, eyes open. Her body, too white.

Too changed.

Only two colors:

    Dirt.

    Blood.

Brown and red fingerprints painted morbid petals across her slashed frame.

So much blood.

Too much blood.

And a word.

He saw it as he bundled her back in the blanket.

        She looked so cold, alone.

        She looked so cold, alone ... dead.

A word carved.

A word carved into a cheek.

FREAK

He touched the leathery lettering. She had left him one last gift. Images flicked through his mind.

Of a man.

Of a knife.

Of Below.

A new emotion began to breed beneath his skin.

Rage?

Yes.

Always.

He tucked her into his bed.

Keeping her safe.

And robotically exited his home and stepped off the edge of the deck.

Dry leaves crunched under bare feet as he landed.

Blood, her blood, had dripped a trail of success that led to Below.

Sol followed. Feet so fast, he flew.

This man was no more. This lover, friend, companion, shelter, home

no longer in existence.

He had died with her.

I will kill you all.

Fourteen

Where the hunters exited, Sol entered. Only one man on guard. Eyes closed, feet propped, watching.

The tall black figure twisted the guard's head.

Off.

Surprise.

No noise.

Only rage. Always rage.

The Other proceeded to the doorway, feeling along the walls as he went.

Blind. *This is how she felt.*

His throat began to descend to his stomach, and he forced it back.

Only rage. Always rage.

He reached the corridor. No one. This was their

night. Their time for rest. He possessed too much power, was possessed by too much fury for their sleeping numbers to affect his plan.

I will help you rest. I will kill you all.

The nightmare drifted from cave to cave. A twisted shadow stealing life.

Collared by loss, led by wrath.

As he coasted through Below searching for more to extinguish,

he smelled it.

He smelled her.

The creature rushed the scent and was greeted by a ticklish laughter.

"I knew you'd come. I could feel it. Just like I felt her."

The glowing figure twirled a blade in his hands and pressed its flat surface hard down his

nose

lips

tongue.

Eyes rolled back with every lick. "That freak."

The word was barely finished, yet the creature had pounced and pinned its prey. The wall of dirt, hard beneath the man's shoulders.

Laughter kept falling.

"It

was

fun."

The Other's grip on the glowing's shoulder squeezed tighter. Thumbs pushed past flesh, muscle, struck bone. "And so is this." The Other unleashed his teeth and tore down the man's face. He ripped through his neck.

Shucking skin.

No more laughter.

Only loss.

Fifteen

lood, death, loss, anguish, rage boiled acid in his stomach. He purged, needing to be empty, and blindly dragged himself back to the opening from where he came.

He again reached the entrance.

It had set her free and now confined him.

The sun was fading, but to this creature, his light was already gone.

He had nothing

and yearned for everything.

A whisper. A name. Floated from the moon and kissed his heart.

Rheena.

Sol stepped into the night.

Hunting Kat

KELLEY

ARMSTRONG

I stretched out on the lounge chair in front of our motel room.

"Basking in the sun, *mon chaton*?" Marguerite's French-accented voice sounded behind me. "You have been doing a lot of that lately."

"Can't get sun cancer now."

"No, you just like thumbing your nose at the myth."

I grinned. "A sunbathing vampire. So Dracula-retro."

She sighed. I tilted my head back to look at her as she stepped out the screen door. Like me, Marguerite is a vampire. She's been one a lot longer, though. Over a hundred years, though she looks twenty, the age when she died. Eternally beautiful. Well, in Marguerite's case, at least—she's tiny with blond curls and big blue eyes. I'd thought she was an angel when I first met her. She was *my* angel, rescuing me from a science experiment and from parents who weren't my parents at all, but people paid to care for me.

That was ten years ago. I was sixteen now, and undead for six months. Marguerite had nothing to do with making me a vampire. That was the experiment, plus a bullet to the heart.

Marguerite had known what I was all along. That's why she'd taken me. She'd never told me the truth, though. I found out the hard way, waking up on a morgue slab. I understand why she kept it a secret—she wanted me to grow up normal—but I haven't quite gotten over it. I don't tell her that. When it comes to feeling guilty, Marguerite doesn't need any help.

"Are you hungry?" she asked, holding out a travel mug.

"Not for that."

She set it down beside me. I could smell the blood, warmed to body temperature. Like that made a difference.

"You need to drink, Katiana," she said.

"It's stale. Now that . . ." I waved at a man three doors down, passed out drunk. "That's a proper breakfast. Not like he'd notice. He's already going to have a killer hangover. A missing pint of blood wouldn't matter."

"You are too young to drink alcohol."

"Ha-ha."

"I am serious, Kat. Whatever is in his blood will be in yours. Drugs, alcohol . . . You have to consider that."

"No, I need to consider what I am. A hunter. I need to hunt, Mags. You do."

"And so will you, *mon chaton*, when you are—"

"Psychologically and emotionally ready." I tried to keep the edge out of my voice. "But you're going to talk about it with the other vamps, right? That's why we're going to this meeting in New York."

"We are going for many reasons."

"But you are going to ask them whether I should start hunting."

"Yes, I will. Now drink. We still have a long drive."

Marguerite went back inside to get ready. I drank the blood. It was like eating store-bought chocolate chip cookies—I could taste hints of what I really wanted, what I craved, but they were hidden under a leaden layer of foul crap.

As I sipped, I eyed the drunk guy and imagined sinking my fangs into his neck. Imagined his blood, hot and rich. The back of my throat ached so much I could barely gag down my blood-bank breakfast.

I know I sound like a coldhearted bitch, fantasizing about drinking some guy's blood, like I'm brutally nonchalant about the whole vampire situation. I'm not. I have my good days. And I have my bad ones, too, when I can't get out of bed in the morning, when I lie there and think and worry.

Am I going to be sixteen forever? Marguerite says no, that the genetic modification experiment was supposed to get rid of the eternal youth thing, which when you think about it, isn't really such a blessing, being one age forever, never able to settle in one place, make friends, get a job, fall in love. . . .

What if the modifications failed? What if I *am* sixteen for the next three hundred years? I think about all the things I didn't get to do before I turned. Things I might never get to do.

Even if the modifications took, how would that work? I can't be injured, can't get sick. Does that mean I'm invulnerable, but not immortal? That I'll die when I'm a hundred, like everyone else? Or will I live to three or four hundred, like real vampires? If I do, will I keep aging at a normal rate, and turn into some hideous old hag? Marguerite doesn't have any answers, just keeps saying it will work out, which means she's just as concerned as I am.

I try not to think about all that. I've got enough to worry about with my life now. Hungering over humans. Drinking blood. Fearing that the Edison Group will find me again. Worrying that I'll screw up and get caught.

Even without the Edison Group problem, there's so

much to stress out about. What if I get hit by a transport and the paramedics take me to a hospital where, whoops, suddenly I'm as good as new? What if people figure out I'm a vampire? Would they kill me? Experiment on me? Lock me up? Would I be any better off than if the Edison Group *did* catch me?

So, no, I'm not nonchalant about it. I'm dealing. Kind of. Today we were heading to New York to meet other vampires and get some answers about the genetic modifications and about how to handle my situation. So today was definitely going to be a good day.

As for hunting humans, I'm not nonchalant about that, either. When the time comes, even if it doesn't have lasting effects on people, I expect I'll feel guilty about it. Marguerite does. But I still need to hunt. I feel that in my gut, a gnawing restlessness, like when I haven't done a workout in a while.

When the feeling gets bad, no amount of canned blood helps. I'll be walking along and I'll smell something unbelievably good. I'll start salivating, stomach growling, and I'll turn to see, not a plate of freshly baked cookies but a person, maybe even a friend. I can't describe how that feels. It's bad. Just bad.

I finished my drink and went inside. Marguerite was in the bathroom putting on makeup. I perched on the counter, watching her as she applied pale lipstick to a mouth that was already a perfect pink bow.

"So who's the hot vampire in New York?" I said. "A tall, dark Napoleonic soldier you met during the Civil War? Sheltered him from the witch hunts? Got separated on the *Titanic*, each floating off on your own icebergs?"

"History is not your strongest subject, is it, *mon chaton*?"

"I'm improvising. So who is he?"

"There is no he. I want to look nice for people I have not seen in a while."

"Uh-huh."

I looked in the mirror—yes, unlike Hollywood vampires, I can see my reflection. Beside Marguerite's fragile porcelain perfection, I always feel big and clumsy. Seeing us together, though, the difference isn't that obvious. I'm only a few inches taller, and skinny enough that I can snag her designer shirts and leather jackets. No one ever mistakes us for sisters, though. My golden brown hair, green eyes, and lightly bronzed skin guarantee that.

I reached for her makeup bag. She snatched it away and handed me lip gloss.

"When you are seventeen," she said.

"I may never be seventeen."

"Then you will have no need for makeup, will you?"

I sighed. Marguerite can be unbelievably old-fashioned sometimes. The perils of having a guardian who grew up in the nineteenth century. On this point, though, I don't really care. I'm a jock, not a cheerleader. Makeup is a pain in the ass. Well, most times. I make an exception for dates. Not that there'd been any of those since I turned. Let a guy nuzzle my neck and he might realize I don't have a pulse. Marguerite says guys won't notice, but I'm not ready to take that chance.

I wandered into the bedroom, picked up the keys and jangled them. "Don't forget I have my license now. Better hurry or I'll go to New York without you."

She didn't peek out of the bathroom. Didn't call after me as I walked out the door. Didn't even ring my cell as I drove our little rental car from the motel lot. She knew I wasn't going far. There are days when I like that, knowing she trusts me. Then there are others when I really wish I was a little more rebellious. A little less predictable.

She probably even knew where I was heading. We'd passed a coffee shop and bakery a few minutes before we stopped for the night, and she'd promised to let me head back in the morning, grab my morning coffee. Vampires don't need food. We can still eat and drink, though, which helps us fit in. For most, like Marguerite, food doesn't sit well in their stomachs. Not so with me. That's one of the modifications that *did* work, apparently.

I grabbed an extra-large hazelnut vanilla coffee and a cinnamon bun. Then I headed back, music blasting, pedal to the floor, zooming along the empty Vermont road. Well, close. I had the music moderately loud and I was going about ten kilometers over the speed limit. Five *miles* over the speed limit, I should say. I'm American, but Marguerite is French Canadian, and we've spent most of the past decade in Montreal, so I'm used to the metric system.

Miles or kilometers, the point was that I wasn't speeding very much, and I left my coffee and bun untouched beside me until Marguerite was driving. Yes, I can act like a smart-aleck teen, but I rarely break the rules. It's my upbringing, Marguerite says. The only time my "parents" ever praised me was when I was a model child, tediously well behaved. Being a vampire doesn't make me a badass. Sadly.

I'm not a complete wimp, though. So when a pickup came roaring up behind me, I didn't follow my driving instructor's teachings and pull over to let him pass. I sped up. He stayed on my bumper, coming so close I could only see his truck's grille.

That made me realize just how empty the road was, winding through the foothills, dense trees on either side, a steep embankment down to my right. I hadn't seen another car since leaving town. Not the place to play road warrior. So I slowed to the speed limit and eased over, giving him plenty of room for passing.

When he made no move to go by, I slid my cell phone

from my pocket. Then the grille disappeared from my rearview mirror as the truck swung into the other lane to pass.

I glanced in my side mirror. It was only a glance. I had both hands on the wheel. I didn't drift into his lane. I was sure of it. But the next thing I knew, there was a crunch, metal on metal, and my car shot toward the embankment.

My throat seized up, brain screeching, brakes screaming along with it as I slammed on the brakes. The car kept going, sailing over the edge.

It rolled and it kept rolling and all I could do was duck, hands over my head, until there was a bone-jarring crash. And everything went dark.

I blacked out for only a second. When I came to, the car was still groaning from the impact. I opened my eyes to see a tree in the passenger seat. The car was wrapped around it.

I reached to undo my seat belt, but I couldn't twist. A branch had gone through my shoulder and pinned me to the seat. I stared at it. There was a *branch* through my *shoulder*. And I couldn't feel a thing.

I took a deep breath, reached up, and pulled it out. Took some effort. Vampires don't get superhuman strength—another myth debunked—and the branch was all the way through the seat, so it required work, but finally I got it free. It left a hole in my shirt, but no blood, obviously. There was a hole in my shoulder, too, but it would seal up.

I tried to check out the damage in the mirror. Seeing myself, I let out a yelp and closed my eyes fast. Another deep breath. Then I pulled down the visor and opened the mirror.

My nose was broken. Smashed nearly flat from an impact I couldn't remember. My lip was split. And one of my eyes was . . . not quite in place.

Oh God. My stomach heaved. I closed my eyes and pressed my palm to the injured eye. It . . . went back in. I shuddered, stomach spinning.

I reached up and straightened my nose. As I moved it, I could feel it reforming under my fingers.

There. All fixed. Now—

"Hello!" a man's voice shouted.

I lowered my head to look out the smashed window. A vehicle was parked at the top of the embankment. The guy who'd run me off the road?

No. It was a car, not a truck. Two sets of legs stood beside it. They must have seen my car fly off the road.

That really wasn't any better. I couldn't let rescuers find me, not while I still had a hole through my shoulder and God knows what other injuries, all of which would miraculously heal during the ambulance ride to the hospital. This was exactly the sort of scenario I'd feared.

I stuffed my cell phone into my pocket and grabbed the door handle. My fingers slipped on the wet surface. Coffee, I realized. The whole interior of the car dripped with it.

Hey, at least it's not blood.

I wrenched the handle. Not surprisingly, the door didn't open. I twisted to get up, so I could kneel on the seat and go out the window.

My legs wouldn't move.

I stared down. They were crushed. Oh God. My legs were *crushed*.

"Is someone down there?" the man yelled.

"I think I see a car," a woman answered. "Have you called the . . . ?" Her voice drifted off.

Okay, they weren't coming down here. Not yet, at least. I had time. I tugged at the broken steering wheel. It snapped off in my hands. I set it aside, then ran my hand down my legs, trying to wriggle them free. The muscles weren't responding, but my legs seemed to be loose.

Just as long as they weren't *really* loose . . . like not connected to the rest of my body, because I was pretty sure that whatever regenerative abilities vampires had didn't go that far. Really sure actually, considering that the only way to kill me was decapitation. Some parts just don't grow back.

My legs seemed fully attached, though. And already mending, which meant in a few more minutes, they'd be *really* pinned.

I ratcheted my seat back and wriggled until I got my legs out. They still wouldn't move, though, which may have had something to do with the broken bones sticking through holes in my jeans.

It was a good thing I wasn't overly squeamish. My dream of a career in sports medicine was looking a little dim these days, but at least my summers volunteering at a clinic came in handy as I repositioned my legs. The bones slid back in with surprising ease, like they were just waiting for a nudge.

They obviously *weren't* going to mend in the next few minutes, though, meaning I couldn't wait to walk away from this accident. I cleared the safety glass from the window, pulled myself through . . . and hit the ground face-first, somersaulting onto my back. I lay there, getting my bearings and listening.

I could still hear the couple at the top of the ridge, but I couldn't make out what they were saying until I caught the words ". . . seems to be a path down over here . . ."

I rolled over fast and pulled myself through the undergrowth. There was no way to do that quietly. Dead leaves rustled and dry brush snapped as I crept forward.

Before long I heard the man shout, "I think someone's down here!"

I dragged myself along faster, watching for the man's head to appear over the long grass. Which meant I *wasn't* watching where I was going. When my hand touched down on air, I tried to pull up short, but it was too late. I tumbled over a stream bank, getting a mouthful of mud and water as I splashed down.

"Did you hear that?" the man yelled.

Running footsteps sounded. I looked around. There was no place to hide. I was trapped . . .

. . . in a swollen, muddy stream at least two feet deep.

I pulled myself into the deepest part of the stream-bed and stretched out. The ice-cold water closed over me. As the water filled my nostrils, some still-human part of my brain went crazy, telling me I was drowning. I squeezed my eyes shut and ignored it.

After a few minutes, I sensed the couple approach. Yes, sensed. Before I turned, Marguerite tried to explain this vampire's sixth sense, and I'd compared it to sharks, who can pick up electromagnetic pulses from their prey. Now that I've experienced it, I'd say that's exactly what it is—a weird pricking of the skin that tells me people are close.

When I concentrated, I could pick up the couple's voices, muffled and faint.

". . . car's empty."

"No one could have walked away from that."

"Well, there isn't any blood. Maybe the driver was thrown clear."

"We'll backtrack. Keep looking. The police should be here any moment."

I waited until I couldn't sense them anymore. Then I lifted my head slowly. I could hear them back by the embankment.

I wiggled my legs. They were moving now. Good.

I tried pushing up. My legs gave way and I splashed back into the stream. I hunkered down, but the couple must not have heard. I rose again, not putting too much weight on my legs, just using my knees to get some traction, pushing myself up the streambed and into the long grass.

When I was far enough away, I took out my cell phone.

It was off. And it wouldn't turn on.

As I shook it, a shadow passed over me. I looked up, and caught only a blur. Then hands grabbed my shoulders and pinned me down. Something ice-cold pressed against my neck. I writhed and twisted, struggling to get free, but the world tilted and spun and then . . .

When I came to, there was still a guy bending over me. Instinctively I jerked up and slammed him with a line drive to the chin. He flew back with a yelp. I jumped to my feet. Still a little wobbly, but at least I could stand.

I glanced around quickly. The forest was gone, and I was in a room with wooden plank walls, like a cabin. I blinked hard, woozy from the sedative, my brain not kicking into gear yet.

The guy I'd hit glowered up at me as he rubbed his chin. He looked about my age. Broad shoulders. Football player build. Dark hair. Blue eyes, which were looking more pissed off by the second. When I stepped forward, he leaped to his feet, fists flying up, boxer stance. I took a step. He swung. I grabbed his wrist and threw him over my shoulder.

"Could I get a little help here?" he called as he struggled up from the floor.

"He'd like you to stop hitting him." Another male voice, lower pitched, with an accent I recognized from a few months in New Jersey. I looked over to see a second teenage guy sitting on a crate, book in hand. Scrawny. Glasses. Wavy light brown hair that tumbled over his forehead. He glanced up from his book, dark eyes meeting mine. "Please."

"Thanks a hell of a lot," the other guy said.

I turned. The jock was coming at me, moving slow, cautious.

"Look," he said. "Whatever you think—"

Another step brought him into personal space range.

Another wrist grab landed him on the floor.

He glared at Glasses. "Would it kill you to get involved?"

Glasses gave me a once-over. "Maybe." He closed the book but made no move to stand. "Clearly she thinks we're the ones who brought her here, which would make sense, coming to with you crouched over her. First, I would point out, though, that we're a little young to be in the market for a backwoods bride. Second, had we been the ones taking her captive, I hope we'd have had the foresight to tie her up before waking her. Third, if she checks for exits, she'll discover we're as trapped as she is."

I looked around. It was a single room with only blankets and crates on the floor. No windows. One door. I walked over to it and yanked. It was bolted—from the outside. I could sense at least one person guarding the door.

I turned back to the guys. The one with the book stood.

"Neil Walsh," he said. "That's Chad. We hadn't gotten to surnames yet. I take it you're a vampire?"

I stared for a second, then choked a laugh. "Excuse me?"

"Vampire. By blood, at least. If not, then you're in the wrong place. This party, apparently, is only for hereditary vampires. *Genetically created* hereditary vampires.

Subjects of an experiment. Escaped subjects, I might add."

If my heart still beat, it would have been racing. "I—I don't know what you're talking about."

"Cut the crap," Chad said. "You'll—"

Neil lifted his hand, stopping him. "It might not be crap. We knew what we were, but she might not." He looked at me. "If that's the case, then ignore everything I just said."

"Oh, that'll work." Chad took another step toward me. "I'm sorry if this is news to you, but as crazy as it sounds, it's the truth. You were part of an experiment. Someone—maybe your parents, like mine and Neil's—took you away from it. The guys who kidnapped us are bounty hunters. My guess is that our families trusted someone they shouldn't have, someone who could be bought. These bounty hunters want to take us back to the scientists. The Edison Group."

I struggled to keep my expression neutral, but there must have been a glimmer of fear in my eyes when Chad said that name, because behind him, Neil nodded. Chad only kept looking at me, waiting for a reaction.

"Okay . . . ," I said finally. "So . . . vampires . . ."

"Not *real* vampires," Chad said. "Obviously you aren't out there sucking blood and hiding in the daylight."

"Real vampires aren't allergic to the sun," Neil said. "The book says—"

"Screw the book. My point is that we aren't vampires. Not yet. Not for a very long time, I hope."

I held myself still, hoping to give away nothing.

"Okay, that's a lot to take in," Chad said. "And you probably think we escaped from the loony bin, but the main thing is that we're trapped and there are others out there, like us, in danger. Two more kids who escaped. We need to get out, find them, and warn them."

I nodded. I didn't dare do anything else.

"You're hurt."

Neil was looked at my legs. I glanced down. My jeans had huge holes where the bones had poked through.

I sat quickly and made a show of examining the skin underneath. "Just ripped. Probably when I was running through the woods. That's how they caught me—ran me off the road."

When I looked up, I almost bumped heads with Neil. He was bent over, looking at my legs through the holes. The flesh was still pitted, the skin rough, like scar tissue.

"Old accident," I said.

He looked at my other leg, with the same circular scar right under the tear. Then he looked at me. I kept my face impassive, but I could tell he knew, and I felt a weird tingling in my chest, like my heart was trying to pound.

Neil nodded and straightened. "As long as you're okay."

"She's *not* okay," Chad said. "She's a prisoner about to be handed over to mad scientists. Same as us. Same as those other kids." He looked at me. "Do you have any idea who they are?"

I shook my head.

He continued. "Maybe you didn't know about the experiment, but you must have heard something. You've been on the run, right? Like us? Did your parents talk about other kids? Maybe you visited them and your folks said they were old friends?"

"No, I'm sorry."

He exhaled, cheeks puffing. "Okay, well, think about that while we work on an escape plan. But don't ask *him* for ideas." A dismissive nod toward Neil, who'd already retreated to his crate. "He isn't interested in escaping."

"Of course I am," Neil said. "As I see it, though, we're temporarily without options. No windows. One door, locked. Presumably the men who brought us here are right outside it."

"They are," I said before I could stop myself. "I mean, I heard someone out there. Or I thought I did."

Again, Chad bought it. Again, Neil didn't, studying me with that inscrutable look.

"Go back to your vampire book," Chad said. "We'll wake you up when we're ready to go."

"Vampire book?" I said.

"It's the journal of a vampire," Neil said. "My parents

told me what I am only last year. They're hereditary vampires themselves but don't know very much about the condition. Entire families carry the gene, but for most members, like my parents, it's recessive."

"Fascinating," Chad said, yawning.

Neil's gaze settled on me, like he was waiting for permission to continue. I nodded, and he did.

"By recessive, I mean that, on death, they won't return as vampires. They may, however, pass that ability on to their children. With both carrying the gene, my parents were concerned it might increase the chance of their child being a true vampire. They were directed to the Edison Group, who promised that with some genetic modification, they could ensure that didn't happen. They lied."

"They made sure it *would* happen," I said. "And they made other changes as well."

"Presumably. My parents left the experiment once they discovered the truth. They did not, however, stay around long enough to learn exactly what was in store for me if . . ." He paused, head tilting. "*When* I become a vampire. Once the bounty hunters discovered how little I knew, they gave me this." He lifted the old book.

"Thoughtful of them."

A twist of a smile. "They're trying to scare me. Show me what horrible future is waiting for me while promising that, despite what my parents told me, the Edison

Group isn't really evil. They can help."

"You don't seem very scared to me."

He shrugged. "Knowledge is power. I want to know exactly what's in store. And, if I'm lucky, there may be something in here that'll help us. Some ability they aren't expecting."

"Well, you go ahead and read that," Chad said. "In the meantime, I'll actually try—"

He stopped and stepped toward me.

"There's a huge sliver sticking out of your shoulder," Chad said. "Didn't bleed though. Weird."

Damn! It must have been left over from the branch. I should have checked better. As I twisted out of Chad's way, Neil quickly slipped behind me and said, "It's the angle of entry. It just didn't hit any veins. Here, I'll take it out for you."

I hesitated, then nodded.

"Are we allowed to ask your name?" he asked as he steered me out of Chad's line of vision and wriggled the sliver free.

"Katiana," I said. "But everyone calls me Kat."

"Katiana. Hmm. Russian?"

I said it was. I had no idea and knew he wasn't really interested in the answer, was just talking to distract Chad, which I appreciated.

"Thanks," I said, when he pulled it out.

He nodded. He had the sliver cupped in his hand and

was tucking it into his pocket. When fingers touched the back of my shoulder again, I spun.

"Hey!" I said.

Chad stepped back, staring at his clean fingertips. "There's no blood." He looked up, gaze hardening. "There's no *blood*."

He grabbed my arm so fast I didn't see it coming. Neil tried to stop him, but Chad wrenched me off balance. His fingers went to the side of my neck. Before I could yank away, he shoved me aside.

"She's a vampire," he said, staring at me like I'd just crawled out of a crypt.

"No kidding," Neil said. "That's why she's here."

"You know what I mean. She's a real vampire. Turned. *Dead*."

"As we'll be one day," Neil said. "And if you're wondering why she didn't tell us, your reaction answers that."

"How the hell can you be so calm? She's a *vampire*."

"At the risk of repeating myself, so are you. She's just a little further along in the process." He glanced at me. "It didn't just happen, did it? In the car accident?"

I shook my head. "It was about six months ago. The Edison Group caught up with us. Shot me, apparently figuring they were safe either way. Either I'd be reborn as a vampire and prove their experiment succeeded, or I'd die and they'd have one fewer escapee to worry about. They didn't get their answer, though. They thought I was accidentally cremated, so they stopped looking for me."

"If the bounty hunters are still gathering escaped subjects, they may not have notified the Edison Group. Which means these men may not have realized you've transformed already. We should keep it that way. It'll be an advantage—"

The dead bolt clicked. The door opened an inch, a gun barrel poking through. A man said something. I didn't hear it. All I could do was stare at that gun, remember the last time I'd seen one, remember the flare, the bullet hitting my chest . . .

Neil's fingers wrapped around my elbow. "Do as they say," he whispered.

Chad was at the far wall, facing it, hands up. We did the same.

"Spread out more," the man said. "Hands behind your backs. Make one move and we'll test whether you really can come back from the dead."

A chuckle from a second guy.

I put my hands behind my back. They bound us, then ordered us out. I caught a glimpse of one captor. There wasn't much to see—just a guy in a Halloween mask. Dracula. I suppose they thought that was funny.

They took us out to a cube van. The back doors were open, the interior empty except for bottled water and old blankets. Without a word, they pushed us inside and slammed the door.

There was only one window—a grimy square on the van's back door. It let in just enough light for us to be able to see one another. Not that anyone seemed very sociable right now. Chad sat in a corner, knees up. Neil was on the other side, back to the wall, staring into nothing, deep in thought. Neither had said a word to me since we got in.

I felt the weight of that silence. From Chad, I expected it. Neil had seemed different, but I guess it had just been logic talking back there. He knew he *should* be okay with me because someday he'd be a vampire too. Now, in the silence, emotion took over and he wanted nothing to do with me.

"I'm sorry."

Chad's voice at my ear made me jump. I looked over to see him beside me.

"I was a jerk back there," he said. "I'm sorry. I just . . . It caught me off guard."

"It's okay."

"It's not, but thanks."

He smiled then, a slow grin that, six months ago, would have had my heart skipping. Now all I could think was how good he smelled. Like dinner.

I looked away.

"There," Neil said, making us both jump.

Neil lifted his hands. The rope fell free. He frowned at the abrasions on his wrists. Blood seeped from one. I could smell it.

"Good," Chad said grudgingly. "Now, can you get ours off too?"

"That was the plan."

As he freed us, I was careful not to inhale. Of course, I still thought about the blood smeared on his wrist. I couldn't help it. That gave me an idea, though. For escaping.

I told the guys. Chad jumped on it. Neil didn't. We talked about alternatives, and he couldn't see one, though, so he agreed.

The van screeched around a corner, bumping along a dirt road as Chad banged the walls and shouted for help. It jerked to a stop. The passenger door opened and slammed. Chad went still, lying on the floor of the van, me crouched over him, mouth hovering over his neck.

I could hear the blood pounding through Chad's veins. Heard it, felt it, saw it, the pulse on his neck beating hard, blood rushing so close to the surface I could smell it. My fangs extended. I pulled back, shuddering, instinctively closing my eyes to focus on retracting them, then stopped. This was the idea, right? Fangs and all.

So I crouched there, over Chad's neck, fangs pressing

into my lower lip, and I tried to look at him, to see him like I would have six months ago, to notice the way his dark lashes curled on his cheek, the sexy hint of beard stubble, the full lips. . . . But all I saw was his blood, pulsing behind his skin, so close I could taste it. God, I swore I could taste it.

A movement to my left. I glanced over at Neil, lying on his side, blood from his wrists smeared on his neck. He was watching me. No expression. Just watching.

I glowered at him and hissed, "Eyes closed!"

He shut them just as one of our captors cleared the filthy window and peered through to see me crouched over Chad.

"Hey!" the bounty hunter shouted. "Ron!"

He threw open the back door and I leaped up, fangs out, snarling. The guy froze, eyes wide, gun still down, like he'd forgotten he had it. I lunged at him. He dropped the gun and fell back, hands flying up to protect his throat.

I sprang on him, pushing him backward. A shout from the driver as he ran around to help. Chad jumped from the van and knocked him down. Neil hopped out behind them.

I pinned my prey to the ground. *Prey.* That's all he was at that moment. I didn't think about what I should do next. I pinned him and I bit him.

My teeth sank in like needles through silk. Hot blood

filled my mouth. And the taste. Oh God, the taste. It was unbelievable.

If he struggled, I didn't notice it. Didn't notice anything until that first mouthful slid down my throat, then the blood-fog cleared and I heard Chad fighting the other guy. My target was out cold. The sedative in my vampire saliva had done its job.

I lifted my head. That took effort. Serious effort, like wrenching myself out of the sun on a bitter cold day. I closed my eyes and ran my tongue over my fangs. They retracted. I didn't straighten, though. Couldn't. Just stared at the blood trickling down the man's neck.

"You need to seal it," said a soft voice beside me.

I glanced up. Neil stood over me.

"The book says you seal the wound by—," he began.

"I know," I said, sharper than I intended.

I shifted so he couldn't see, bent, and ran my tongue over the puncture wounds. The holes closed. The bleeding stopped. I could still taste the blood, though, so delicious it made the back of my throat ache.

"Katiana?" That same soft voice. Careful, like he didn't want to disturb me.

I straightened, grunting, "I'm good."

With my back still to him, I swallowed. Ran a hand over my face. Squared my shoulders. Turned around.

Chad knelt beside the unconscious body of the other man.

"Good," I said. "We need to—"

Neil held out the ropes that had bound us earlier.

"Okay," I said. "Let's do that."

Soon our captors were bound and unconscious. Now that I could get a look at them without masks, I knew I'd never seen them before. Just two guys in their twenties, both dark-haired and broad-shouldered. There was a definite resemblance between the two. Brothers or cousins, I was sure.

They were incapacitated, though, and we had their van and keys. So our next move should have been obvious. It would have been, if one of us knew how to drive stick shift. We tried, but no one had been driving more than a few months. We just didn't have the skills to manage it.

Neither of our kidnappers had a cell phone. One had a radio, but that meant they weren't working alone, and we sure weren't going to let their partners know that we'd escaped.

There was only one option. Walk.

First, Neil went back and grabbed the gun. There was only the one, and when Neil brought it over, Chad put out his hand.

"Can you shoot?" Neil said.

"Better than you."

Neil raised the gun and put a bullet in each of the

van's front tires. Chad scowled, walked away, and waved for us to follow.

The van had pulled off onto what looked like an old logging road. We'd been on a paved one before that. We found that quickly. It was ten minutes, though, before we heard a car. Even then we couldn't see it. We were on a thickly wooded road that bounced through the hills of Vermont. Or I presumed it was still Vermont.

When we heard the car, Neil suggested we get off the road, so it didn't barrel over the hill and send us flying like bowling pins. We stayed at the side, ready to wave it down.

As it drew closer, Chad said, "Maybe this isn't such a good idea."

I glanced at him.

"Well, those guys had a radio, right? That means they're working with others. Maybe they were supposed to hook up. Or maybe those guys have escaped already, and called for help. Even if it is someone else, do you think they're going to stop for us? Or will they call the cops?" When neither of us said anything, he shrugged. "Okay, I'm just putting it out there."

"What do you suggest?" Neil said.

"My folks are back in Pennsylvania. Yours are in New Jersey. But Kat's are close by, right?"

"My guardian is." I'd been trying not to think about

Marguerite, how worried she'd be. I knew she'd be look-ing for me—I only hoped she was safe.

"Then I say we get off this road and keep walking until we come to a town and can call Kat's guardian."

We agreed and moved into the woods before the car reached us. It was a mom with a couple of kids in car seats. Not a potential captor, but probably not someone who'd stop, either.

"So you and your guardian . . . ," Chad said. "You were traveling somewhere? That's what I overheard them saying before they grabbed Neil. They sent some-one up to Quebec for you, but then their contact said you'd headed this way. They found and followed you."

Neil added, "And presumably kept following you until the van could intercept you after kidnapping me."

"Were you taking a trip?" Chad asked, ignoring Neil.

"Meeting others in New York," I said.

"Others?"

"Vampires," I said after a moment. I braced for his reaction, but he seemed interested now, like he'd gotten over that initial knee-jerk response.

"And your guardian knows them from the experi-ment? Maybe the other subjects who escaped will be there." He grinned. "That'd make things easy."

I shook my head. "We didn't even know that others had left the experiment. I was taken out when I was five."

"But this guardian of yours, she was in on it, right?"

"No. She's . . . she's a vampire. There was this group of supernaturals who were concerned about what the Edison Group was doing. They were secretly monitoring the experiments. She was assigned to me. When she saw how I was being treated, she took me."

"*Abducted* you?"

"It wasn't like that." My voice carried a bit of snap. Time to change the subject. I turned to Neil, who'd been walking silently beside me. "So where'd you learn to shoot?"

"A co-op placement at our local police station. They threw in sessions on the firing range as an incentive. I can point and shoot, but that's about it."

"More than I can do," I said. "Very cool. So—"

"Co-op with the cops?" Chad cut in. "What were *you* doing there? Fixing their computers?"

"Don't be a jerk," I said.

"I'm not. It's a serious question. Bet I'm right, too. You gotta admit, he's the type."

"And what type would that be?" Neil said. "The type who can *spell* computer?"

"Okay, *not* cool, guys," I said, lifting my hands. "You two have fun insulting each other. I'll be back here."

I slowed to let them get ahead. They kept walking, shifting farther apart. Neil glanced back, like he was thinking about coming back with me, then settled for falling behind Chad and forming a single line. No one spoke for about five minutes. Then Neil cleared his throat.

"I think we should split up," he said. "We have no idea if the nearest town is twenty miles this way. Or five miles back the way we came. Or one mile up that road we just crossed."

"I don't think—" I began.

Chad cut me short. "You've got a point." He stopped and looked around. "Kat can keep going this way. I'll head back. You can take the side road."

I shook my head. "And what do we do when one of us finds a town? We don't have any way to keep in contact."

A valid argument. Neither guy listened, so I had them memorize Marguerite's cell number and walked away.

As I trudged through the forest, I cursed Chad and Neil. Was it just me or was this the stupidest idea ever?

As pissed off as I was, though, I couldn't help wondering if this separation was my fault. Maybe I should have kept my mouth shut when they were sniping at each other. Of course, that would have required industrial-strength duct tape. We'd just escaped bounty hunters. We were running—well, walking—for our lives. And they thought slinging insults was a useful way to pass the time?

No, I couldn't have kept quiet. If that made them decide to split up, then it was a seriously lame excuse.

Maybe that's what it had been. An excuse. Not to get away from each other, but from me. Put some distance between themselves and the bloodsucker before she gets hungry.

It didn't matter. I'd get to a town and I'd call Marguerite, and if the guys were worried about hanging out with vampires, they could call a ride of their own. I'd never see them again. Which was fine. Not like they were my new best buddies or anything.

It had been nice, though, finding other kids from the same experiment. Other vampires. Only they weren't vampires. Not really. But I guess, in a way, I'd liked the idea of meeting someone who kind of knew what I was going through, who—

I sensed someone close by. Really close by. I wheeled as Neil jogged through the trees. He held up his hands, the gun still tucked in his waistband.

"It's just me," he said.

"Did you find something?"

"No." He waved for me to follow. "Come on. We need to get in deeper before they get here."

"They're coming?" I said as I followed him. "Did you tell Chad? We need to—"

"We need to stay as far away from Chad as possible, considering he's the one who called them."

I stopped. "What?"

He reached for my elbow and tugged me into the

forest. "He's a plant. I suspected it from the start, but I'm sure now. He's gone to call them. That's why he wanted to split up."

I jerked out of his grasp. "No, you wanted to split up. It was *your* idea."

"My thoughts exactly," said a voice beside us.

Chad lunged from the bushes and charged Neil. He grabbed for the gun, but only managed to hit Neil's arm. The gun went flying. I dove for it. We all did. I was faster, though, and snatched it up, then backed away, gun wavering between the two. They froze.

I looked down at the gun in my hands, and again, I remembered that fatal shot. But this time the memory passed with only a spark of emotion.

"Who suggested splitting up?" Chad said after a moment. "If there's a plant here, it's obviously him."

"I suggested it to smoke you out," Neil said. "Splitting up was a stupid idea. Katiana knew that. But you were all for it . . . because it gave you the excuse to call the bounty hunters."

"Call with what?" Chad lifted his arms and turned. "Pat me down, Kat. I don't have a phone."

"Because you hid it as soon as you overheard me. Katiana, you know he's not a vampire. Look at how he reacted to you. He showed no interest in the book. He's shown no interest in what your life is like or what you're going through. That's not the reaction of someone who expects to become a vampire."

"Maybe because I'm scared, okay?" Chad said. "Can I admit that? Or do I have to be all logical about it like you? To me that proves you *aren't* one. You're overcompensating, making sure we know you're okay with it."

"He's a plant, Katiana. He was the first one picked up—"

"Which would be a dumb idea if I was in on it. The smarter move would be to grab me second, to throw off suspicion. And who says there's a plant at all? Where did this idea come from? What possible reason would the bounty hunters have—"

"First, as a precaution against exactly this scenario—we escape. If one of them is with us, they can make sure we don't get very far. Who's the one who didn't want us flagging down a passing car?"

"But I didn't suggest splitting—"

"Second, they don't know where the other subjects are. They assume we do. You've been very curious about those other subjects, Chad. We gotta find them. *Gotta* find them. And, by the way, do we happen to know where they are?"

"Enough," I said. "Neil has convinced me . . . that there is a plant. Makes sense. The question is, who?" I stepped forward, gun pointed at Chad. "One way to find out if you're a vampire, isn't there?"

"Whoa!" Chad backpedaled. "Vampire or not, I

wouldn't want that. Come on. Obviously, it's him. He's the one who wanted to split up."

I turned the gun on Neil. He paled. Sweat trickled down his temple.

"All right," he said. "I'd really rather not, but if that's what it takes, go ahead. I'd only ask that you let me turn around and aim for the base of my skull. It's the quickest way to kill someone."

"What the hell kind of freak knows that?" Chad said. "Sure, let him turn around . . . so he can run away as fast as his scrawny legs will take him."

Neil turned. I could see the side of his neck throbbing as his heart raced. He didn't even shake, though. Just stood there, waiting. That took guts. Incredible guts.

I swung the gun back on Chad. He dove at me. I could have shot him. But I wouldn't, not while I had any other option. So when he came at me, I dropped the gun, grabbed him by the wrist, and threw him.

Before I could pin him, he flipped over, a hard elbow to the jaw sending me flying off my feet. It took me a second to recover. As I did, I heard a grunt and a thump behind me, and when I turned, Chad had the gun—and Neil, holding him as a shield, one arm around his neck, gun barrel pointed at the side of his skull. Neil's glasses were gone, lost in the scuffle.

Neil said, "Considering I just *agreed* to be shot, this really isn't the position of advantage."

"Shut up, freak."

"Keep calling me that and I might take offense."

Neil's voice was steady, jaunty even, but sweat still slid down his face, and I could see that pulse in his throat.

"Let him go," I said.

"Or what? You'll bite me? Feed on me?" Chad's lip curled in undisguised disgust, and that answered my question better than any test I could have given him.

"You aren't a vampire," I said.

"No, thank God."

"But you are part of the experiment, I'll bet," Neil said. "You're the right age, and that's the most obvious way you'd know about it. What are you?"

"Half-demon."

"I'm sorry."

Chad's arm tightened around Neil's neck. "You think I'd want to be a bloodsucker? Goddamned parasites should have been wiped out centuries ago."

"I didn't mean that. I was expressing my condolences on your status as an experimental failure. Your lack of powers."

Chad's eyes blazed. "I have powers, smart-ass. You want to see them?"

He closed his eyes, face going rigid as he concentrated. I charged. I smacked the gun from his hand and knocked Neil free. The gun sailed into the bushes. Chad and I hit the ground. He grabbed me by the shoulders.

I felt his hands through my shirt, felt them heat and smelled scorched fabric. But that was it. As powers went? Kind of sad.

Chad threw me off. When he came at me, I kicked, and sent him flying, then leaped to my feet. We circled each other. He glanced over at Neil, who hadn't moved.

"Letting a girl fight your battles?" Chad said with a sneer.

"She seems to have it under control."

"Coward."

Neil shrugged.

Chad threw a punch at me. I caught his arm and flipped him. He leaped up and charged. I kicked and knocked him into a tree. He staggered up, shaking his head like he was dazed, then rushed me. I spun out of the way, but he caught me by the arm and yanked me off my feet. Then it was my turn to meet the tree.

"Need help?" Neil called as I recovered.

"Nope," I said.

Chad and I went a few more rounds. I had the advantage of skill—I'm a second-degree black belt in aikido and a brown belt in karate, from self-defense training that Marguerite had insisted on. He had size, plus a generous dose of real-life brawling experience, it seemed, which I definitely lacked.

The advantage swung slightly my way, but not enough to make it a quick or easy fight. We'd been going at it for about five minutes—which feels like fifty when you're actually fighting—when Chad threw me down hard. I lay there, winded.

At a grunt behind me, I jumped up, thinking he'd gone after Neil, and found Chad face-first on the ground. Neil had one knee on Chad's spine, Chad's arm wrenched behind his back.

Chad tried to buck Neil off. Neil twisted his arm until Chad was the one with sweat streaming down his face. He didn't take it as stoically as Neil had, though. He snarled and gasped as Neil kept inching Chad's arm up. Finally Chad stopped struggling.

"I don't suppose you'd care to tell us anything helpful," Neil said.

Chad spit out a string of curses.

Neil glanced at me. "Does that sound like a no?"

"Sure does."

"Do you think we're likely to get anything from him?"

"Nothing useful," I said. "I think we can guess the story. The guys who captured us are relatives. They kind of looked like him. Same build. Same coloring. They know about the experiments because he's a subject. They got a lead on us, probably, like he said, from someone your parents and my guardian have stayed in touch with. Rather than turn that information over to the Edison Group, they figured they could make some money rounding us up. Only they're missing a couple of names, so they recruited Junior here to play captive in hopes of getting those names from us." I bent beside Chad. "Am I close?"

"Go to hell."

I turned to Neil. "We can ask whether he's contacted his coconspirators yet, but either way he'll say he has, just to freak us out, hope we'll take off and let him go."

"You're right. There's nothing we can get from him." Neil backed up a few inches, making Chad wince. "I can knock him out, but your method seems safer."

Chad struggled again then. It didn't do him any good. A little more pressure on the arm and Chad was screaming. A quick bite on the neck and he stopped screaming.

This time, though, I forced myself to stop as soon as blood filled my mouth.

"You're hungry," Neil said as I rose from Chad's unconscious body. "You should drink more. If the book is right, he'll only wake up weak, as if he donated blood. It's not like he doesn't deserve it. And there's no sense turning down a free meal."

How many times had I given Marguerite crap for ignoring an opportunity to eat? Or told her off for trying to hide her feeding from me? Rolled my eyes and said she was being stupid about it. She had to eat and I understood that. Just consider it a blood donation to save a life—hers.

Easy to say when you're on the other side. But crouching here beside an unconscious kid, even a jerk like Chad, while having another guy watching you, a guy who wasn't a jerk, but maybe someone you'd like to impress . . .

"I'm good," I said, rising.

"Katiana . . ."

"I don't feed like that. I get my meals from the blood bank."

He frowned. "The journal says vampires need fresh—"

"My guardian doesn't want me to hunt yet."

"Okay, but you didn't hunt him, so . . . I mean, if you don't want to, sure. It just seemed, back there, like you *did* want—" He flushed. "Sorry. I'll shut up now."

He knelt beside Chad and started patting him down for a phone. Neil had a point. It wasn't like Chad didn't deserve to wake up feeling like hell. This was what I'd wanted, right? Not just drink a single mouthful, like I had with the other guy, but to take a full meal straight from the source, see if it made any difference. See if it dulled the edge.

But I couldn't do it. I don't know if it was the thought of feeding off someone I knew or of doing it in front of Neil. I wanted to—oh God, I wanted to—but I couldn't.

When I glanced over at Neil, he was holding his glasses. It looked like they'd been a casualty of my bout with Chad, stomped underfoot.

"I knew I should have worn my contacts yesterday," he said, trying for a smile.

He ran his hand through his hair, shoving it back from his face as he squinted and blinked. Without glasses, Neil wasn't magically transformed into a sex god. He just looked a little less like a guy who should be planted behind a computer monitor and a little more like one who could manage a first-rate throw-down and pin. Definitely cute though—with or without the glasses.

I shook the thought off. Really not the time for that.

"Can you see?" I asked.

"Well enough." He tossed the glasses aside, retrieved the gun, and held it out. "You may want to be in charge of this, though."

"Can you still shoot?"

He shrugged. "Sure, but—"

"Can you avoid shooting figures with brown hair, blue jeans, denim jackets, and"—I looked down at my feet—"dirty white sneakers?"

A genuine smile. "I can."

"Then keep the gun. I have no idea how to use one. Now we should see if Chad did ditch a cell phone. It's a long shot, but we need to head back to the road anyway. Maybe we can find his trail."

* * *

We did. It wasn't hard. Chad was no backwoodsman, and we didn't need to be trackers to find his trampled path through the undergrowth. I followed a detour where he'd walked deeper into the brush, then returned, and at the end of that path, under the bushes, I found a phone.

"Do you think there's anything I should know about using it?" I asked Neil. "Maybe a GPS that needs to be disabled?"

"My tech skills are limited to being able to turn things on and operate them. In other words, zero on the geek scale."

I glanced over at him. "I wasn't assuming. I was just asking."

"Did I sound defensive?"

"A little."

A rueful smile. "Sorry."

I turned the phone on and waited to see if anything would happen. Then I checked for outgoing calls. One had been made twenty minutes ago. Damn.

Before I called Marguerite, I needed some idea of where we were. Neil thought he'd seen a sign on the side road he'd been supposed to take. We found a path heading in roughly the direction we needed to go. Once we found the sign, which promised a town two miles away, I dialed Marguerite's cell number. On the second ring she answered with a wary, *"Allo?"*

"Miss me yet?" I said.

"Katiana! Where are you? What happened to you? Are you all right? Are you hurt? They called, the police, about the car. The accident. I said the car was stolen, but I have been looking everywhere, calling everyone—"

"I'm fine. Just kidnapped by bounty hunters rounding up missing vamps from the experiment."

A pause, then, "That is not funny, Kat."

"You think I'm kidding? I wish. I'm with another guy they grabbed. Neil . . ." I tried to remember his last name. "Walsh. Neil Walsh."

"Actually, it's Waller," Neil said. "Walsh is the name my parents have been using since they left the experiment."

Marguerite overheard and said, yes, she remembered Neil. She warned us not to call his parents on the phone we'd found. If it was owned by Chad, our captors could check their billing and which numbers we'd called. I hadn't thought of that. Neil agreed. We'd get to the town and lie low until she could pick us up. Then Neil could notify his parents from a pay phone.

As we walked, Neil fussed with the gun, taking a better look at it and checking the ammunition, saying, "If those guys find us, we might actually need to use it."

"I'm sorry about earlier," I said. "With Chad. I wouldn't have shot you."

"You needed to see how we'd react. While I'm not eager to be turned, I'd rather do that than go back to the Edison Group. My parents told me . . . things." He let the word drop, heavy, and stared at the gun, lost in thought. Then he turned it over in his hands. "It appears to be police issue."

"Is that a problem?"

"Only that it may mean we're dealing with someone who knows how to fire a gun significantly better than I do."

"We'll be fine. You've got some killer aikido skills to fall back on. Speaking of which . . . That might be a popular choice with cops, but there's no way you picked that up in a co-op term. What level are you?"

"In the black belts."

I had to press him for more than that, and after some waffling about nonstandard terminology, he admitted he was fourth-degree.

"Seriously? I just made third. Damn."

"Sorry."

I laughed. "Is that why you didn't want to tell me? You think I'd be pissed because you're a higher level? It just gives me something to strive for. Can't have a guy beating me."

I grinned, and when I did, he gave me this look, like . . . I don't know. He just stared at me. Then he glanced away fast, cheeks flushing.

"Any other martial arts?" I asked as we walked.

"Just that. I'm not much of an athlete, but I like lunch."

"Huh?"

"In fifth grade we moved to a new city and there was this kid, a head taller than me. He decided my lunch money was a good way to supplement his income."

"And you needed a way to keep it."

"Yes, but I prefer using my head to my fists, so I thought I could outwit him by brown-bagging it. He took that. I switched to health food. He'd still take it . . . and throw it in the trash. So, I could either humiliate myself by digging through the garbage every day or learn a form of self-defense. I did my research. Aikido seemed a good choice for what I wanted and, as you said, it's popular with law enforcement, which is a bonus."

"That's what you want to be? A cop?"

He studied me, like he was trying to see if I was mocking him. That was getting annoying. When he saw that I was serious, he said, "A detective. That's what I'm good at—problem solving."

He asked about my meeting in New York, carefully though, like he didn't want to pry. I explained and said he should talk to his parents, see if they could come. He might not be a vampire yet, but if they weren't sure what lay in store for him, this would help.

"I'm sure they'll agree," he said. "They want to help me, and I think it would be good to keep in touch." He paused. "Not that I expect—" He cleared his throat. "I understand that under the circumstances, we've been thrown together, and while I'd like to go to this meeting with you, I know it won't be *with* you."

"English translation please?"

Another throat clearing as he pushed low branches aside. "We got caught up in this together. We pooled our resources to get out. But once we *are* out . . ." He raked his hair back again. "I'm not one of those guys who thinks that if the popular girls ask for homework help, it means they want to hang out after school."

"What's that supposed to mean?"

"I'm just saying . . ." He trailed off, starting and stopping a few times before glancing over, dark eyes meeting mine. "I think you know what I'm saying, Katiana."

"I sure as hell hope not, because it sounds like you're saying that after I've used you to escape, you expect me to walk away, pretend I don't know you."

"You didn't use me."

"Whatever." I turned in his path, facing him. "You're saying you know my type, which apparently means you know *me*. That's rich, coming from the guy who got his back up when I asked if he knew about cell phone technology. Hell, I'm not even sure I have a type any-more, unless you've met a whole lot of teenage vampires."

"No, I do believe you're the first."

He smiled, but I wasn't buying it, and I sure as hell wasn't returning it.

"Maybe *that's* the problem," I said. "Not that you think I'm some dumb jock who wanted your answers on the escape-from-evil quiz, but because of what else I am. Not exactly sure you want to hang out after school with a vampire."

"Of course not. I—"

"I make you nervous. You're trying to hide it, but you can't help it. I get that. I expect that. Just have the balls to say so instead of laying down the post-escape ground rules before we even get to the post-escape stage."

He opened his mouth. I wheeled and stalked off.

"Katiana," he called, as loudly as he dared.

I kept going, walking fast, branches whipping behind me. He started coming after me, but after a minute, his footsteps stopped. I wasn't surprised.

I shouldn't be too hard on him. Can't blame a guy for not wanting to get chummy with a parasite. At least he'd made the effort, which was more than I could say for Chad, and probably more than I'd be able to say for most people I'd meet in my life. Marguerite had two sets of friends: temporary ones who didn't know what she was, and other vampires. This was just the first lesson in a class I'd be taking for a very long time, so I'd better—

A crack sounded behind me. Not a "branch underfoot" crack, but one that sent my insides ramming up into my throat. I spun just as another shot fired. Something buzzed past my ear. A bullet embedded itself in the tree . . . where my head had been just a second ago.

I hit the ground. Even as I dropped, I knew it was the wrong move. Bullets can't kill me. Not lead. Not iron. Not holy-water-blessed silver. Don't duck and hide. Move!

I scrambled into the undergrowth as another shot whizzed past.

Who—? Okay, that was the stupid question of the week. Who was shooting at me? The guy with a gun and, fortunately, without his glasses.

I should have known. God, I should have known. Chad was right. Neil had been too calm about the whole vampire situation. Completely cool with it . . . right up to the moment when he decided to get twitchy and send me stomping off.

If he wasn't with the bounty hunters, though, who was he? What did he want with me? Did it matter? Not when there were bullets whipping past my head. I didn't want to think of what kind of condition I'd be in, waiting for my brain to heal after getting a chunk blasted out.

I crawled along the ground as quietly as I could. The shots stopped. Silence fell as he listened for me.

I'd been raised for situations like this. Sad, I know, being prepared for a life that might involve bullets, bounty hunters, and unlawful confinement. But Marguerite had known what I was in for, and not preparing it for me would be as neglectful as not giving me a warm jacket for a Montreal winter.

As much self-defense training as I had, though, she'd drilled in one lesson above all others: Fighting back was a last resort. Whenever possible, run. For once, though, I had no intention of taking her advice.

I'd already been duped by Chad. Blinded by a desperate need for validation, for the friendship of kids who knew what I was. So I'd missed the signs with him, and now, even worse, with Neil. I wasn't letting him get away with it.

So I circled back in the direction of the gunfire. After a few minutes, I caught a whispered voice. Neil on a cell phone? I hoped so, but when I heard a second voice, that hope fizzled.

If I faced more than just Neil, I should run. But I needed a closer look first. Needed to know what I was up against.

When I was close enough to see figures, I found a suitable tree and climbed. I'm good at that. I used to think I'd turn out to be a werecat—hence my nickname. Obviously not, but I'm still a damned fine climber.

I got high enough to be safe, then shimmied along a branch until I could see three figures. Two men I didn't recognize, plus Neil. They were talking to him. I strained to listen. When I couldn't hear anything, I inched out a little more. Then a little more.

The branch groaned. I froze. Neil's gaze lifted. Our eyes met. His lips parted in a curse.

"What?" one of the guys said.

"Shot," Neil said, quickly looking away. "I said I think you must have shot her. She's gone for help." A glance up my way and he said, louder, *"Gone for help."*

He shifted, and I realized his arms were *bound* behind his back.

Well, that changed things. As much as I'd love to swoop in, be the hero, save the guy, I wasn't an idiot. Two armed men versus one sixteen-year-old girl? Martial arts expert or not, the odds weren't far enough in my favor to risk it. Better to get Marguerite for backup.

I retreated along the branch. It creaked . . . and this time, both men heard it.

A gun swung my way. I jumped to the next tree. I managed to catch a branch. Then my weight hit, and the branch gave a tremendous crack.

I dropped square onto one of Neil's captors. He went

down, me on top of him. Neil kicked the other guy in the back of the knees. He toppled. Another bone-crunching kick in the jaw sent him reeling back.

My opponent had fallen easily, but he wasn't staying down. We rolled on the ground—him trying to grab his gun, me trying to sink in my fangs—then both achieved our goal at almost the same time. His weapon of choice was faster. Mine was scarier, and when my fangs sank in, he panicked, firing wildly, the bullet zooming past my arm. It was the last shot he fired.

Neil's match was giving him even more trouble. Having both hands tied behind your back can do that. I took over. It was a short fight. All I had to do was flash my fangs, dripping blood, and you'd have thought I was a thousand-pound tiger with canines big enough to rip off his arm. The guy backpedaled. Neil kicked the gun out of his hand. I leaped on him. Game over.

As I rose from sedating the second guy, Neil said softly, "Why?"

"Because they're assholes," I said as I walked over to untie him. "Greedy assholes."

"That's not what I mean."

He gave me a look that said I knew what he meant— why wouldn't I feed?

I looked down at the unconscious man. Why indeed? Here it was—my last chance to see if it made a difference.

With Chad, I could say that I didn't like the idea of feeding on someone I'd met. Didn't like the way it smacked of revenge. Really didn't like the way it made me exactly the kind of bloodsucking monster he'd thought I was.

But why not these guys? Because I didn't want Neil to see me? In those few minutes when I thought he'd betrayed me, I'd realized how badly I'd wanted him to be okay with me, with what I was. For someone my age to say, "I know what you are and I don't care."

Was this how I was going to live? Ashamed of what I was? Compelled to hide the worst of it, even from someone who knew the truth? No. I was still the same person I'd always been, and if people like Neil couldn't handle the uglier parts of my new life, there was nothing I could do about it. Nothing I *should* do. What happened to me wasn't my fault.

"I should," I said.

"Yes, you should."

"Will you—?" I cleared my throat. "Will you watch? I mean, not *watch*, but watch him, make sure he's okay. Make sure I don't . . . overdo it?"

"Good idea."

I crouched over the guy, then maneuvered so Neil could monitor his vital signs while not seeing me drink. Awkward. Silly, too, and as soon as I started to drink, I forgot that. All those glasses of warmed-over blood were like day-old doughnuts. This was what I craved. What I needed. It wasn't just a meal. It was . . . I don't know how to describe it. Like eating the best food imaginable, while curled up in the most comfortable chair, listening to my favorite music.

I was so caught up in it that I stopped thinking about being careful. This man under me wasn't a person. Wasn't even food. He ceased to exist. I was swept away by the experience, and when that finally ebbed, and I realized what I was doing, I jumped back so fast that blood sprayed from his jugular.

"Seal—!" Neil began.

I bent and licked the wound. Under my tongue, I could still feel the guy's pulse beating strong. I listened to his breathing, then lifted his eyelids as Neil said, "It's okay, Katiana. I was watching. He's fine."

It felt like I'd been drinking for hours, but the guy barely even looked pale. I exhaled in relief.

"Better?" Neil said.

I nodded, then wiped my mouth and made sure my fangs had retracted.

He crouched in front of me, coming down to my level. "What I said earlier? I didn't mean to piss you off. I was just . . ." He rubbed the back of his neck. "I've been that guy before—the one who thinks that if a girl's being nice and asking for homework help, it means something.

I got burned and I don't like getting burned, so now I cut them off at the pass."

I lifted my gaze to his. "Bet you missed out on a lot of girls who *did* want to get to know you better."

"Maybe."

"Probably."

His gaze dipped, cheeks flushing, and I saw the blood rushing to his face, saw his neck pulsing, heart rate picking up, and I felt the urge to lean forward. Not to bite him, though. There wasn't any of that now. I didn't see food. Didn't smell food. Didn't sense food. I saw Neil, and all I thought about was leaning forward and kissing him.

I didn't. Oh, I would, when the time was right, but that wasn't now. At this moment, all that mattered was that I could look at him and see a cute guy and feel the same way I would have six months ago.

When I smiled, he said, "What?" and I said, "Nothing," and pushed to my feet, and before I could say anything else, a car rumbled past.

"Think that's our ride?" I said.

"Hope so."

"One way to find out."

I took off running and reached the edge of the woods just in time to see a rental car pass, a familiar blond head over the driver's seat. I put my fingers in my mouth and whistled. The brake lights flashed. Then the reverse ones came on, dust billowing as the car sped backward.

Marguerite barely put it in park before she leaped out. She ran over and hugged me so tight I swore ribs cracked.

"Ack!" I struggled to get out of her embrace. "Good thing I don't need to breathe."

"Are you okay? What did they do to you? Are you hurt?"

"I'm a vampire, Mags. I can't get hurt." I waved at Neil stepping from the bushes. "But if you really want to mother someone, he'll be my stand-in today."

"*Allo*, Neil," she said. "I am sure you do not remember me, but we have met, many years ago."

"Good," I said. "Saves on the introductions. I invited Neil and his parents to come to New York with us. Hope that's okay."

"Of course. If he would like that."

Neil's gaze flicked my way, then back to Marguerite. "I'd like that."

"All set then," I said. "You two can get caught up while I drive to the nearest pay phone."

"You are not driving anywhere, *mon chaton*. Not for a very long time."

When we reached the car, I looked back at the way we'd come, toward the clearing where we'd left the two bounty hunters. Back to where I'd fed as a vampire for the first time.

"It's okay," Neil whispered as we climbed into the backseat.

I nodded and smiled. It wasn't quite okay yet, but it would be. For the first time in six months, I was sure of it.

Lilith

FRANCESCA
LIA BLOCK

The wild beasts of the desert shall also meet with the wild beasts of the island, and the satyr shall cry to his fellow; the screech owl also shall rest there, and find for herself a place of rest.
—Isaiah 34:14

Lilith

*P*aul Michael had always wanted to escape.

He shuffled along in the hallway with his hands hanging at his sides, his back bent under the weight of his backpack. He hadn't washed his hair and it was greasy—pieces falling in his face—and some girls in math class had been making noises about how he smelled. Sometimes he didn't take a shower on purpose, just to see them squirm. He really didn't care what they thought of him. He was dreaming about the planet he had created, Trellibrium, where the mighty Norser was defeating the evil forces of Kaligullo to save princess Namalie Galamara. Beautiful lights shone inside Paul Michael's head. He didn't need these kids, this school. He had something better.

But it wasn't always enough. Sometimes Paul Michael

got lonely. He wanted someone to share the other world with. He wanted a girlfriend.

The other thing he wanted, if that didn't work out, was to leave the planet, because it sucked.

Lilith, the new girl, was walking down the hallway toward him. Her steps were somewhat tentative, as if her feet were too small for the rest of her. Paul Michael noticed this because he kept his eyes on the ground. She wore black boots, and their heels clicked lightly against the brown linoleum with its shiny streaks. He could also see her legs, which were long, and her hips that switched gracefully in a predatory, feline way.

Lilith was not like any of the other girls at school, Paul Michael thought. No one knew where she had come from. She had black hair and dark, thickly lashed eyes. She had small, high breasts; but it wasn't only that she was beautiful. She didn't care what anyone thought of her. She always wore a big hat in the sun and covered her skin under black clothes. She hung out alone, strumming her guitar on a bench by herself. She drove a big old black Mercedes, and the rumor was she lived in it. She was freaky and knew it and was proud. Paul Michael believed that if he ever got to talk to her about Trellibrium she would not laugh or roll her eyes or walk away but might actually be interested. She might actually listen.

Paul Michael.

He heard his name, but he didn't actually hear it. It was a sound in his head. And it was in a voice he recognized from the time he had heard it last week, when he ran into her in the principal's office where they were both receiving lectures on something. It was Lilith's voice. As if she had spoken telepathically, like they did in Trellibrium.

Paul Michael stopped and reached for the amulet he wore around his neck. It was carved with the image of three archangels. Paul Michael's mother had given it to him.

"To protect against evil spirits," she said.

Paul Michael tugged at the chain, hard enough so that it broke. He threw the amulet into the trash can. Then he took off his glasses, pretending he just needed to rub his eyes, and looked up to meet Lilith's gaze.

She tossed a smile at him like you would give a dog a bone. Her sharp incisors showed, and her lips were the kind you would never see out here in Nowhere unless you were looking at a movie star on the cover of a *People* magazine in the 7-Eleven.

Someday, her voice said in his head, before she was gone.

Paul Michael and his mother lived in a small plywood house with cactus in the front yard. She was a nurse at the local hospital and worked nights mostly. Paul Michael's mother was so good at taking care of other people that no one thought twice about whether she took proper care of her son. He was strange; Paul Michael knew that was the consensus. She did her best, but he was just strange. Maybe he inherited it from his father, the neighbors speculated. There were rumors that he was a Satan-worshipping speed freak who had left Paul Michael's mother while she was pregnant. He was probably in jail somewhere, everyone said. And his demon seed would grow up to be just like him, probably. *The poor mom*, they said.

Paul Michael trudged down the sizzling road to the school. The days were long and hot, and he spent them dreaming of the planet Trellibrium. Now he was dreaming about Lilith, too. Maybe he would see her later.

At lunch, Paul Michael sat pretending to write about Trellibrium in his notebook, but he was actually watching Lilith. She sat cross-legged under one of the few jacaranda trees that had been transplanted onto the campus, wearing—in spite of the heat—a black turtleneck tunic, leggings, and boots and playing her guitar. She looked as cool as if the temperature was thirty degrees lower than it was. Her dark hair fell over her face so that Paul Michael could only really see her small, fierce chin, her movie-star lips, and a bit of her high, pale cheek. Her fingers, with their chewed-on, chipped-black-polish nails, were long on the guitar strings, and Paul Michael imagined them touching him. He had washed his hair carefully and applied deodorant for the first time in a few weeks. He was even wearing a fresh T-shirt.

Carter and Kirk walked past him, and Carter spat on the ground near Paul Michael's shoe. A little spittle flew and sparked white on the scuffed brown leather.

"Lookin' good, man. You actually took a shower," Carter said.

Kirk snorted. "I don't smell him."

"Got a girlfriend or something?"

Paul Michael scribbled furiously in his book, just nonsense words in tiny, unreadable script. In Trillibrium the princess Namalie Galamara had fallen prey to the evil Pharmatrons.

Carter and Kirk wouldn't leave. They were smaller than he was, but Paul Michael knew they could smash his face if they wanted. He forced himself to look up and saw Lilith watching him. Almost imperceptibly, she nodded her head. Had he imagined it? His heart jolted blood through his veins.

Was she?

Yes.

Lilith was standing. She took her guitar off and left it on the grass. She put on her black sun hat and dark glasses. She was coming over. Carter and Kirk looked at each other, laughed nervously. Lilith kept stepping along in that precarious way on her black suede boots. She stood in front of the boys. Carter and Kirk moved back away from her. She ran her fingers across Paul Michael's scalp, took the long strands in her hand and gently pulled so that his neck fell back and he looked up at her. His eyes were blue with pinprick pupils, and hers were very dark, ravenous.

Carnivorous, Paul Michael thought. *She has carnivorous eyes. Black moons.*

In Trellibrium, Norser prepared to rescue Namalie.

I'm coming for you, Lilith said. *Soon.* Then she added, *You don't have to be afraid.*

He hadn't really heard her voice, but he knew what she had telepathically communicated, the way Namalie "spoke" to Norser. Paul Michael felt the transplanted grass under his fingertips, tugged at the blades the way Lilith tugged at his hair.

Eventually the grass would die too. It wasn't supposed to be here either.

Succubus

$\mathcal{P}$aul Michael lay in his bed in the dark. He had fallen asleep thinking about Lilith. She had run off after tugging on his hair like that, and he hadn't been able to speak to her anymore.

"Come in," he said aloud in his sleep. He was known to say things in his sleep and even to get up and walk around sometimes. Once his mother had found him naked at the foot of her bed, staring at her in a way that she said turned her blood to blue ice. So she gave him the pendant with the archangels and started locking her bedroom door at night.

He felt a pressure on his chest and opened his eyes with a gasp.

Lilith was squatting on his chest, balanced on her feet on the bed with her elbows on her knees and her hands cupping her chin. He realized he had never seen her skin under all the clothes. It was so white that it glowed a pale blue. She had a long neck, long, graceful arms, and a delicately formed collarbone that looked like a bird in flight. Her black eyes were staring hungrily at him, and her teeth were bared. She shifted her weight and drummed lightly on his Adam's apple with her long fingernails. She bent over him and swayed so that her shiny black hair caressed his face.

It was hard for Paul Michael to breathe. He struggled to move, but she had him pinned. His hands grabbed at her legs—the flesh of her calves was cold and covered with small bumps. He ran his fingers down and felt her feet on either side of his torso. They were even colder and had a rubbery texture. What felt like webbing connected the toes.

"What are you?" Paul Michael asked. It was as if she had come down from outer space (maybe from Trellibrium?) to rescue him. He was still having trouble breathing, but he was not afraid. He was suddenly hard, and all his extremities tingled. He felt—what was it he felt? He felt lucky. He felt chosen.

"What do you like best?" Lilith said. "Queen? Beautiful Maiden? Storm Demon? Wind Demon? Succubus? You tell me."

"You are a goddess," he whispered, and she leaned over and pressed her teeth against the vein along the side of his neck, leaned in hard and sweet until the skin ripped and a bead of blood burst forth.

A vampire? Paul Michael thought. But not like the ones in the books all the girls in his school carried around like bibles.

"I'm just going to have a little this time," she told him. "And you'll have just a little too. Then we'll do it again." She paused and wiped the blood from her mouth. "Maybe at Kirk's party this weekend?"

Paul Michael closed his eyes. When he woke the next morning, there were a few black feathers in his bed and blood on the sheets and on his mouth.

Geek

He decided to go to the party, even though it was at Kirk's. Paul Michael needed to see Lilith. And after the other night he felt different, braver and more intuitive. Had she done this to him? Could vampires do that? He tried to recall what he had read about them in comic books and seen in horror films. He thought so. . . .

The party was at a ranch house with a pool where kids splashed in a haze of aqua blue light. Paul Michael got beer from the keg and looked around for Lilith. He saw only Carter and Kirk.

"Look who crashed the festivities!" Kirk said.

"He's probably looking for his girlfriend," said Carter, and Kirk sniggered. "Fat ass really cleaned up his act. I even think he's losing some of that paunch."

Carter smacked Paul Michael in the gut with the back of his hand, and Paul Michael bent over as the pain flashed through him. He had lost weight. He had hardly been able to eat since Lilith had come to his room, but he didn't feel hungry or weak at all. If anything, he had felt stronger until Carter slammed him like that. That strength was because of her, Paul Michael was sure, vampire or no.

He wished for a second for the archangels on the pendant his mother had given him, but they hadn't really helped in the past. The only thing that had helped was Lilith. Maybe she had bitten him like a vampire, but she was the closest thing to an angel he'd ever come across, inside his mind or out.

She was standing outside the sliding glass door by the pool, and lozenges and trails of blue light trembled over her skin. All she wore was a thin black satin dress that looked more like a slip, and she had her boots on. He felt a tremble of desire go through him because he was the only one there—he was sure—who knew what was under those boots. It wasn't gruesome to him. He knew her intimately. He knew her secret.

Carter saw Paul Michael and Lilith looking at each other. He said to Paul Michael, "You know where the word *geek* comes from? You must know, right? Geek?"

Kirk laughed, sputtering beer down the front of his shirt.

Carter snapped his fingers at Kirk without looking back at him. "Go get it," he said.

Kirk ran off and came back holding a sack. It was making squawking sounds and writhing. Kirk opened the sack and handed the chicken to Carter. It flapped its wings in terror and tried to wrench away. Carter held it by the neck.

"What does geek mean, Kirk?" Carter asked like a maniacal teacher.

"It means someone who bites the heads off live chickens," Kirk answered obediently. He went behind Paul Michael and grabbed his arms. Paul Michael struggled, but Kirk was stronger than he looked. His ropy arms held fast.

Paul Michael thought he might vomit. He wanted to look over at Lilith, but he kept his eyes on the ground. Kirk jerked him back, and his glasses fell off. They lay near Carter's sneaker, ready to be smashed.

Carter held the chicken up in front of Paul Michael so he could smell it, and its feathers flapped against his face. He tried to move away, but Kirk still had him like that.

"Bite," Carter said. He reached into his pocket with his free hand and pulled out a pocketknife. He held it up to Paul Michael's throat. A few people had gathered around, laughing nervously.

It was hard to tell if it was the chicken or what, but

Paul Michael felt something swoop down, scratching his face, and then Lilith was there.

Someone screamed.

"You have no idea," she said, in a voice much deeper and lower than what should have come from the throat of a seventeen-year-old girl, "how big my mouth is. I could take your head off in one bite."

She grabbed the knife out of Carter's hand so swiftly and with so much force that he backed away and the bird fell to the ground and flapped in the dirt.

Then Paul Michael broke free of Kirk and she reached for his hand, took it, and began to run. Paul Michael heard a soft shattering sound as his glasses crunched under his feet.

They ran for what felt like a long time, but Paul Michael wasn't really tired. He thought he might be getting stronger. It was almost like flying.

When they got to the highway, he started to cross, but Lilith pulled him so his back pressed against her breasts. He turned his head to look at her and a car roared by, speeding crazily out of nowhere from around a bend. For a moment he saw her lit up in its headlights.

"Look both ways," she told him.

She was so beautiful, he thought. He would do anything for her.

They crossed. There was a dry creek bed along the

road and a beat-up old black Mercedes parked at the side. They went under a chain-link fence, and she led him down into the creek. It was usually full with water from the mountains, the only proof in Nowhere that the white-capped peaks were real, even in the valley heat. They lay down there, among the river rocks and dirt, looking up at the stars in the sky.

"Why did you want to go to that party?" he asked.

She laughed. Almost coyly. "It's practically foreplay to watch those pricks acting out like that."

He took Carter's knife from her hand. She had been clutching it the whole time.

"What are you doing?" she asked softly, smiling.

He lifted his hair up away from his neck—thinking he would have to cut it off, it got in her way—and exposed the tendons to her. Then held up the knife to his neck. She laughed.

"I don't need that, silly," she told him.

Of course, Paul Michael thought. *Duh. Can you say teeth, Paul Michael?*

When she pulled away from him, his neck was throbbing and her mouth was black with blood in the dark.

"Your turn," she said.

The Rescue

There was only one more time.

He woke in the middle of the night knowing he had to go to her. He got into the shower and scrubbed his skin with a rough washcloth until it almost hurt. Got out, wrapped a towel around his waist, shaved. Then he took a pair of scissors and cut all his wet hair off, shaved the remaining hair with his razor. There were a few nicks on his scalp that he dabbed at with bits of toilet paper. He put on a white undershirt and Levis. The jeans were loose—he'd lost weight in his gut. He didn't put on his glasses. They were broken, gone, lost in the dirt, and he didn't need them anyway. Paul Michael went outside and began to run. Suddenly he realized he probably shouldn't have taken so much time getting ready.

He found her old diesel Mercedes parked by the

riverbed. Carter and Kirk's bikes were nearby, and the trunk of the car was open.

He walked up so quietly, amazed at how light and quiet his step had become, and saw what was happening. Carter and Kirk were bent over the trunk. He could see past their shoulders—his eyesight even in the dark and without glasses was different now. They were staring at her legs, and her legs and feet were bare. Paul Michael felt the violation of their eyes on her strange legs and feet. He took Carter's knife out of his pocket, grabbed Carter by the collar, and pulled his head back so his throat was exposed. Kirk stumbled back and began to run, and Lilith opened her eyes and smiled at Paul Michael. He lunged into Carter, pushing his teeth into Carter's neck, just breaking the skin a little. There was blood, and he moved back and bowed his head toward Lilith, who came forward and bent to drink like a little girl at a drinking fountain, demurely tucking her hair behind her ears. Paul Michael heard a soft gurgling sound. The taste of Carter's blood was still salt and sticky on his lips, and he didn't know if he could get used to drinking as much as he might eventually need. But he wasn't all the way there yet, anyway. Lilith had said it was going to take a little while. She finished with Carter and mounted him the way she had mounted Paul Michael in his bedroom, but this time doing something complicated and quick to his neck and then tossing him aside onto the dirt. His body looked like a stuffed SpongeBob Paul Michael had as a kid after the dog ate all its stuffing. Lilith looked up at Paul Michael and her face was radiant, her cheeks and lips plumped up and her eyes bright. She grabbed him by the back of his neck and kissed him, sliding her mouth down over his chin and clamping her teeth into his neck. He was instantly hard. This time she drank for a little longer. He felt long, slow waves of pleasure, as if she was touching him below the waist. When they were done, she took the knife and made a suicidal slash across her wrist. She offered it to him, and he tenderly tasted the droplets, then lapped thirstily as more came out. When he was done, he watched as the cut sealed itself up without a mark.

He looked up at her and she glowed, infused with moonlight. "What do we do now?" he asked her.

She tilted her face to the sky, cupped her hands around her mouth, and made a strange, shrieking sound. They waited.

The birds came out of nowhere in the dark, a huge flock of black carrion birds that swept down upon Carter's body, tore it to shreds as Paul Michael and Lilith watched, and spirited it away without a trace.

"What about Kirk?" Paul Michael said. "He'll get help. Someone will come."

"He didn't make it home." She squinted into the sky after the last bird. "There will be an investigation eventually, but for now I have time."

They got into the back of her car, and Paul Michael told her all about Trellibrium. She listened carefully, asking pertinent questions.

"So Norser rescues the princess?" she asked.

He nodded, stroking her hair.

"But they should rescue each other," she said.

He smiled to himself in the dark. There was a long silence. Paul Michael thought he could hear the stars crackling in the sky.

"What about you?" he asked her. "I want to know all about you. Where you come from and why you are here and how you became what you are."

She sighed. "It's better for you to know me only as I am, without the weakness I had before, to inspire you."

"I want to know everything."

Lilith turned on her side and leaned her head on his shoulder. She felt small as he cradled her, not like someone who could kill a boy the way she had.

"I was just a girl," she said. "I thought I was really ugly. These boys were constantly calling me names. I was sexier than I should have been; I made them uncomfortable. So I turned all that power on myself. And that power—that girl sex power—it's hard-core. I was going to kill myself, and I could have easily done it, and then this person came into my life. I called him Adam. He made me into this so that I could have my revenge and so that I could be his forever. But after he made me I was even more powerful than he was, and when I took my revenge on the ones who had hurt me I hurt him, too. Because I didn't want to belong to anyone."

Paul Michael didn't feel that way, not at all. He wanted to belong to Lilith. She shifted and extricated herself from his embrace, then reached up and placed her own small arms around him.

After a while, he fell asleep like that. Hers.

Black Moon

*T*he next morning, when he got home, Paul Michael looked at himself in the mirror, but he was not there. He was not there at all. He looked down at his arm. His skin looked smooth, hairless, and almost shiny. Paul Michael touched his face. His skin felt smooth there, too. No blemishes, no sheen of oil. He didn't need his glasses anymore; he had left them smashed in the dirt the night before, and that was where they belonged. When he touched his scalp it was baby smooth. He lifted his arm and sniffed his armpit. There was no scent. None at all. Except perhaps a very faint tang of iron and something floral, maybe violets or white roses or poppies. He smelled beautiful. He smelled like her.

Later, after he had slept, Paul Michael left the house and walked into the night. It was a bit cooler, always after the sun had set. A warm wind swept through the town. It was riddled with disease and miracles. There was no moon. Black moon time. Lilith called it that.

Paul Michael's step was lighter. He almost felt like he was floating, as if he didn't have any organs weighing him down. The streets were mostly empty. A few cars drove by, and Paul Michael found himself retreating into the bushes, away from their light. He didn't want the light, but he wasn't afraid. That was one big difference; he wasn't afraid of anything anymore.

But he was hungry.

His veins ached. They felt shrunken and thirsty. He looked down at his arm again, and he couldn't see any veins showing through the skin at all. He pumped his fist and there still wasn't anything.

"Paul Michael."

He heard her voice, but in his head, so he wasn't sure if she was there or not. "Lilith?"

"I've come to say good-bye."

She was standing before him. He reached out and tried to touch her, but she turned just in time and he missed. She glanced back and smiled. Her teeth were razor-sharp pearls.

"You will take my place."

"Why me?" he asked, thinking of all the hot, sexy, strong boys she could have chosen.

"Because I need you to."

"But why did you choose me?"

"Because you were the one who wanted to escape the most. Out of all the lost souls everywhere, I sensed the power of your imagination, and of your need."

He remembered, for the first time since it had happened, the abyss of Carter's eyes, the hell of them. Paul Michael would be a killer now, and, if Lilith left him, always completely alone.

He wondered if it was a punishment or a gift, what she had given him.

An owl screeched, from the dark air, a sound much worse than sudden, violent death, like the destruction Paul Michael was now condemned to visit upon the world.

He had no way to ask her. She was gone.